S

OF

GRACE

Book Six of the Grace Series

M. Lauryl Lewis

DEDICATION

For Rooney and Bubby, because you both are also so very brave. And for Riko, because you are forced to be the bravest of us all.

FROM PRAYING FOR GRACE (#5):

The next four hours were the best I had slept in months. Gus woke me as soon as Hope began to stir. At first, I feared he was waking me to tell me that she had passed away, as Molly had. Seeing the fear in my eyes, he quickly calmed me.

"It's ok, she's just waking up hungry," he said as he smiled down at both of us. "Laura brought in some old towels that she cut down to use for diapers. I've already changed her."

Our new baby had one eye open and was smacking her lips hungrily. I touched her cheek lightly and she turned her face toward me in search of a meal.

"She needs a bath," I said gently as I smiled at her.

"I'll ask Laura to warm some water while you feed her."

"Gus?"

"Ayup?"

"Thank you."

"For what, darlin'?"

"For her. For you. Just for everything."

"You're welcome. I'll be back in a few minutes, okay?"

"Ok."

He left the room to find Laura, and I adjusted myself in the bed, sitting up so that I could hold Hope to my breast. She was warm and making soft little noises as she searched eagerly. One of her little hands caressed my breast as she suckled. I slipped my thumb under her palm and looked at her pudgy fingers. Her skin was soft. Everything about her was amazing. Everything about her was good, in a world full of bad.

Before long, Laura and Gus came back to the family room. They both smiled at the sight of me and the baby. I couldn't help but smile back.

"Everyone else is asleep," said Laura. "I heated water in the kitchen so both mama and baby can get cleaned up. Gus can help you while I get a proper bed ready for you guys."

"Thanks Laura," I said quietly while Hope continued to feed.

"I also left some rice and meat on the kitchen table for both of you. You'll need it to get your strength back."

"Can I ask you one more favor, Laura?" asked Gus.

"Anything."

"Do you mind holding the baby so I can get Zoe taken care of first? I don't want her getting up alone for the first time in case she's weak."

"Do I mind?" chuckled Laura. "I'd be thrilled to hold the little one."

***

Gus helped me to the bathroom, where I was able to do my private business and shower. Even though the water was cold, it felt good to rid myself of the mess of birth and hours of built up sweat. Once I was done, Gus set me up at the kitchen table, where I began eating the food that Laura had left out for us. Gus excused himself to get Hope, saying he'd eat later. I was pretty sure the meat was rabbit that had been stir fried with fresh vegetables from her garden. I hadn't realized that I was as hungry as I was until I began eating.

Before long Gus walked in, carrying Hope in his arms. He looked like a natural.

"Someone's ready for her first bath," he said.

"Is Laura coming in?" I asked.

"Nah. She headed back to bed. Poor thing was exhausted after everything today."

"She's sweet. I really like her."

"Yeah, me too."

I stood and joined Gus by the sink, where a pot of hot water had been cooling. It was just warm enough for Hope's bath. He asked me if I wanted to bathe her, but I declined. She was too new, and too small. I was afraid I'd hurt her. Instead, I watched

3

as he gently poured warm water on her and followed with soap. She cried when he rinsed her off.

I walked beside him as he carried her down the hallway, wrapped in a towel, to the bedroom that had belonged to Alice. It was still the middle of the night and dark, but Laura had left a couple of candles lit beside the bed. Gus laid Hope down on the bed and finished drying her off. She was still pink, but clean now. Her head was covered in fine white hair. In looking at her beautiful eyes more closely, I realized that her tiny eyelashes were white as well.

"Gus, why's her hair so light?"

He sighed. "I've noticed it too. We'll need to watch her, but it might be albinism."

"Be what?" I asked, being unfamiliar with the term.

"An albino. Her eyes are so light, and her hair."

"What if she is? What does it mean?"

"Worst case scenario we need to keep her out of sunlight. Possible blindness down the road."

I climbed onto the bed and leaned over Hope, kissing her on the head.

"I'll love her no matter what."

"She'll be ok."

I knew he couldn't promise that.

***

The next weeks passed as the six of us got to know each other better. Hope worried us constantly as her growth continued at a rapid rate. She ate almost non-stop and at almost a month old looked and acted at least twice her age. It was clear by now that she indeed was albino, as Gus had thought. Her hair was fine as silk and white as can be, and her eyes remained pale blue. She seldom cried or fussed and brought joy to us all. She didn't appear to have any health issues, and seemed to be thriving. Gus and I each felt a connection to her on the deep level that we connected with each other. Sometimes, I'd hold her as she slept and I could feel the emotions of her dreams. Hoot quickly took on the role of uncle, and Laura and Clark were thrilled to treat her like a grandchild. It wasn't the family I had imagined having one day, but I was thrilled to have them all in our lives.

Laura and I spent most of our time in her garden, which now included an expansive green house that Gus and Hoot had made out of logs from the nearby forest and clear plastic sheeting that Clark had left over from when they had first built the house. We hoped it would work well enough to provide fresh produce through the coming winter. Laura was teaching me how to can fruits and vegetables, as well as fish that we caught from a nearby stream. We had no plans to leave the little concrete house built into the hill. It was home now. It had been weeks since we had seen any of the dead. Or the living. Still, we lived on edge, always expecting the worst.

Four weeks to the date after her birth, Gus and I vowed to love and cherish each other, along with Hope, in front of our new family. We celebrated with homemade wine and a wild roast turkey that was stuffed with cornmeal, potatoes, and herbs.

ONE YEAR LATER

Our first winter was tough on us all. We lost most of our garden when snowfall collapsed one end of the greenhouse. Luckily, Laura and I had done a significant amount of canning and Hoot and Gus kept a makeshift outdoor cooler full of small game. Summer brought with it new hope as the surrounding land began to thaw. Our daughter was nearly a year old now, but the size of a two-year-old. She had learned to walk, but was still a bit unsteady on her legs. She hadn't uttered a word yet, but loved to laugh at her daddy. Her eyes remained a shade of blue paler than the sky and her white hair had grown to her shoulders. Luckily, she didn't seem bothered by the sun despite her pale skin.

"You ladies ready?" asked Gus, staring at us from the open doorway of our bedroom.

I smoothed the knee-length patchwork dress that Laura had made for Hope out of scraps of fabric she had lying around and patted her bottom as she toddled toward her dad.

"All ready," I said with a smile.

"Laura packed lunch," Gus said as he scooped Hope into his arms. "Can you say 'lunch'?" he asked her.

She responded by giggling at him.

"That's Daddy's big girl," he said as he gave her a kiss on her pale cheek.

"I'll be right behind you," I said.

"We'll wait for you by the front door."

"Ok."

It was our first big outing, all six of us together. Laura preferred to stay close to home, but Clark had talked her into joining us on a brief hunting expedition disguised as a picnic. Hoot and Clark packed rifles in the off chance we came across any big game, or the dead.

The air outside the home was crisp and fresh. The sky was blue and a gentle breeze blew. We hiked for almost a mile. Hope insisted on walking part of the time, but Gus carried her as much as she'd allow.

We stopped to eat lunch in a meadow bordered on one side by the edge of a glacier. Hope refused to eat anything but the chocolate chip cookies that Laura had baked that morning. She was busy playing in the nearby wildflowers while the rest of us ate roasted marmot that Clark had shot just the day before. It had been so long since I had felt the dead inside of my mind that I didn't realize it wasn't Gus or Hope I was feeling. By the time I was aware of the creature's hunger, Hope was almost to it. I stood, dropping my plate of food, and began to run toward her.

"Hope!" I screamed.

My little girl turned to look at me, and then looked away. My stomach dropped in fear. I could sense Gus close behind me. I could sense his thoughts. How could we have let her go so far… Panic set in as Hope quickly approached the edge of the glacier that sat across the meadow. That's when I first saw it. It looked like half a man. It was reaching toward her, but not advancing. At first I thought it was missing its lower half.

"Hope! Stop!" I screamed shrilly.

To my horror, she continued toward the creature. It wasn't approaching her and appeared to only be a torso, which was oddly upright. I could feel its hunger in my head. The familiar hunger of the newly risen. Its only goal was to feed, and it wanted my daughter. It craved her flesh in a way that I had never felt one of the dead crave flesh before.

"Hope!" screamed Gus, who I sensed only steps behind me.

She reached the creature only a couple of yards before we could get there. It reached its arms toward her in desperation. She stood before it, seemingly unafraid. The dead man dropped his arms as she took two final baby steps toward him. It seemed transfixed by her eyes. She reached one of her pudgy hands out and touched him on the forehead.

"Bye-bye," she said suddenly. Her first words.

Gus passed me in his rush to reach Hope. He scooped her up and swung her away from the threat, holding her close.

I looked down at the Roamer, who was now slumped forward and lifeless. His lower half was frozen in the ice.

"Holy shit," said Hoot as he reached us. "What the fuck happened?"

"Bye-bye," said Hope with a giggle, struggling to get out of Gus' arms. He refused to let her go.

"It must have thawed," I said.

I no longer sensed anything from the creature. I kicked at its head with my foot to make sure it was really dead. Its head fell backward. The creature's left cheek was bruised and scuffed. Its left arm was twisted unnaturally, making me think its shoulder may have been dislocated at some point. The right side of its beige winter jacket had a label that said "Steve."

"That's mountain climbing gear," said Gus, pointing to a pick axe frozen in the nearby ice. "He must have frozen up here, poor fucker."

"Hope? Did you do this?" I asked her.

7

"Ma-ma. Bye-bye," she muttered, pointing to the dead and still-half-frozen man.

My eyes filled with tears, hearing her first words. I reached up and touched her cheek gently. She shared with me her deepest thoughts, not using words. Our child had killed the creature with her touch. She knew it was evil. She knew she was here to rid the world of them.

STATE OF GRACE

CHAPTER 1

Only two of us remained from our original group; a fact that was still so very hard to swallow. Hoot joined us just before we lost Boggs. My heart still ached daily at the loss of my best friend. Hope was already sixteen months old, and the size of a three-year-old. Accelerated growth seemed to be her "norm." Gus tried to convince me to not worry. *Tried* being the key word.

Winter had been hard on all of us, but especially Laura. Despite having the cooking stove in the kitchen and the open fireplace in the middle of the living room, the cold constantly crept into the mountain home into which she and her husband, Clark, had welcomed us. Laura's arthritis worsened with each passing month. Food stores quickly dwindled and Laura lost weight faster than the rest of us. She was thin to start with, but became nearly skeletal by the time spring arrived. Clark doted on his wife, but his face became creased with worry as time passed. Gus was still my knight in shining armor. Our bond with each other was as strong as ever, seemingly amplified when Hope was near. Hope. She was the joy in our lives. Not just for myself and Gus, but all of us. She seldom spoke, but emanated joy all around her. Her pale skin and white hair and eyelashes remained as fair as the day she was born. Her eyes were light but had darkened a bit and she showed no signs of visual deficits. She was able to tune into our emotions easily. The green lines that had riddled my leg, abdomen, and neck while pregnant with her had receded back to my hip, but the light lines that had mingled with them during my pregnancy remained. They were the same shade of pale as my daughter's skin.

As spring arrived, preparations began for venturing out and away from our hillside home. We were critically low on supplies, and the decision to leave was made after many nights of sitting around the fire discussing options. Leaving during the freeze of winter was out of the question, as snow was too deep and temperatures far too cold. We had gone months without seeing any of the dead, which could only assume was a result of the bitter cold. One of the last Roamers we had seen was down a few hundred feet in elevation and had frozen stiff, literally. As badly as we all wanted to stay in our "Hobbit House," we knew there was no way to scavenge enough supplies and pack them in before the next winter would hit. The only drivable road had washed out when fall hit the year prior. While we attempted to grow and preserve our own food, our garden had failed and the remaining growing season was too short to sustain all six of us. The mountainous land around us was rocky and hard, far from being fertile farmland. Hunting provided us with protein, but animals were scarce. Like humans, their populations also dropped when the dead rose. The only option that made sense was to trek back to the lowlands, where unfortunately the dead were surely waiting.

CHAPTER 2

"Hope, it's time," I called out softly to our daughter as she sat quietly on the floor playing with blocks that Clark had hand carved out of wood.

She looked up at me, her face serious and unsmiling. She knew I was afraid.

"Put your blocks into their bag, sweetie," I encouraged.

"No, Mama. Stay," she babbled.

"No, we have to go. Remember? To get more food?"

She shook her head back and forth, her loose white curls bouncing. "No, Mama. Bad. Bad."

"Gus!" I called out, perhaps louder than necessary. "Hope needs you!"

"Coming, darlin'," he called back.

I continued packing Hope's clothes into a tote bag that Laura helped me sew. It had a wide opening and a long strap to comfortably wear over my shoulder and across my chest. It was large enough that Hope herself could sit inside if need be. We wouldn't be taking much, just what clothes we could manage to layer on ourselves, dried venison, water, and weapons. And, of course, Hope's favorite wooden blocks and a small rag doll that Laura made with love.

I smiled when Gus walked into the room, which caused Hope to do the same.

"Da-da!"

"Hi baby girl," he said, greeting her.

I loved watching him interact with our daughter. They shared a very special love that warmed my heart.

"No bye-bye," she said with a pout.

"Aw, baby girl, we have to go on an adventure. It'll be warmer where we go, and we'll find more food."

She reached her arms up toward him and he leaned down and swooped her up.

"Daddy will keep you safe," he added.

I prayed he would be able to make good on that promise.

He planted a kiss on her pudgy cheek and she leaned into his chest.

"I think everyone else is ready, darlin. What can I help with?" he asked me.

"Hope needs to put her dress on over her pajamas, and then her jacket."

"I'm on it," he said softly.

"She should wear her bonnet to help stay warm."

"I'll have Laura help with that," he said with a smile.

"Thanks. I'm almost done packing. I hate to leave this place, Gus."

"Yeah, me too. Some good memories here. Right, Hope?" he said, trying to make himself sound chipper.

Hope's only reply was to turn her head and slip her left thumb into her mouth as she snuggled against her father's chest.

***

Hoot took the lead as we left our home behind. It was still early morning and the air was crisp. Snow surrounded us, but was slushy from the season beginning to change. Hope clung to Gus, who wrapped his free arm around her. Each of us carried a bag or pack filled with supplies. Each of us also held a melee weapon and four of us had firearms. Laura's fingers were too twisted and painful from arthritis to fire a gun. We agreed that if we were to encounter the dead in numbers too large for comfort, she would take Hope and position herself in the middle of the rest of us. It would give her something to do while the rest of us handled the weapons.

Hope was aware of what the living dead were. Born into a world ruled by them, it's all she'd ever known. Just how deep that awareness was, well, a guess. She had only encountered three of them in her lifetime.

As we walked away from the place that held so much security over the past year and a half, my head was blissfully clear of signatures of the dead. I could sense Gus' love for me and for Hope, and I could feel Hope herself deep in my core. She was worried, and sleepy, and wasn't sure if I had packed her dolly.

Gus, hold up for a minute.

I spoke to him silently, and he quickly stopped and waited for me to catch up. I pulled Hope's doll out of my sack and tucked it under her arm. She grabbed onto its white yarn hair with her little fist and held it to her nose as she sucked on her thumb. I could feel her anxiety slip away and she closed her eyes and fell asleep. I kissed her cheek before we began walking again.

Laura and Clark were several yards ahead of us, with Hoot immediately in front of them.

Let me know if you need me to carry her.

"Ayup," he answered verbally as he winked at me. "I will. Don't plan on it though because she's keeping me warm."

I smiled back at him as we continued on. The sun was finally the trees, causing some of the slush-puddles nearby to release tendrils of steam. The air smelled dank and of plant rot. Not particularly unpleasant, but earthy. The snow was thinner amongst the trees, making our descent in elevation easier than it might have been. Water dripped from tree branches, making plopping sounds as they hit the earth. Aside from that and our footfalls, it was eerily quiet. Hope slept on Gus for the next few hours. We stopped at one point to fashion a sling around his shoulder, across his chest and back, and nestled under her bottom to help lessen the strain on his arms.

"Hoot," called Gus only loud enough to grab the other man's attention.

Our friend, still in the lead, stopped and turned to face us.

"What's up?" he asked

"I think we should break for twenty."

I picked up on Gus' reasoning, silently. I looked toward Laura, and saw that she was leaning on Clark. She was looking

14

in Gus' direction and appeared grateful for the suggestion of stopping. The worry lines on her face were a testament to how difficult life had become in the past year and a half.

"Sounds fair," answered Hoot. "Everyone should grab a small snack and get off their feet."

I walked closer to Gus and began helping him free Hope from the makeshift sling.

"We're going to stop for a bit, Sweet Pea," I whispered to her as she stirred awake.

She nodded sleepily. The fair skin of her face was blotchy from the cold, and I began to second guess our decision to leave the mountain before spring was in full force. Gus sensed my concern and placed one of his large hands on my shoulder.

We'll be ok once we get lower in elevation.

I smiled uncertainly at him. Hope reached her arms to me and clung to me as I took her from Gus.

"Let's find a place to go potty," I whispered to her.

With a lack of disposable diapers and frequent laundering not being practical, we had potty trained her early. Still, she was young enough to need reminding to avoid an accident.

She hesitantly removed her thumb from her mouth and whispered to me. "I wanna go home."

I gave her a quick hug before setting her down on the ground and simply ran my hand over her bonnet reassuringly. I took her tiny hand in mine and walked with her to a small clearing between evergreen trees. As she finished going to the bathroom, I began to pull her homemade tights up when we felt the ground tremor. It was so slight that at first I thought my legs were just shaky from miles of walking. Within seconds I could hear a low rumble that matched the growing unease beneath our feet. Hope sensed my fear, as clearly evidenced in her eyes. The ground continued to roll, and by then I knew it was an earthquake. Instinctively, I pulled her close and covered her with my own body. She cried as Gus rushed to our side, shielding us both with his larger frame. The tremor stopped before I could count to twenty.

"Are you all ok?" called Hoot from several yards away.

Gus stood up, allowing me to straighten. I took Hope's hand in mine and looked to the rest of our group.

"I think we're all ok. Just a bit shaken," answered Gus. "Pardon the pun. You all ok?"

"Fine," said Laura with a quiver in her voice.

"I haven't felt one that strong in years," said Clark.

"Daddy? Up? Up?" Hope was reaching her hands upward, and Gus lifted her into his arms.

"It's ok, Buttercup. Every now and then the earth shakes a bit. We'll be ok."

"I know," she said simply before nestling against his chest.

I wondered if she really did know.

"Let's get out of here," Hoot's voice boomed from a few yards away.

Gus and I walked to him, concerned by the alarm in his voice.

"What is it, brother?" asked Gus.

Clark and Laura joined us. No words needed to be said. We all followed Hoot's gaze to the peak of Mt. Rainier, where a plume of dark gray smoke rose angrily toward the sky. The meaning didn't set in until I picked up on Gus' silent worry. Hope's breathing quickened as she sensed our combined fear.

"Break's over," said Gus quietly to our daughter. "Hold on tight, ok?"

Hope stuck her thumb in her mouth and nodded.

"I'll take her for a spell," offered Hoot. "Let's put some distance between us and that bastard."

Clark looked at Laura, the love in his eyes reflected back by hers. They grasped each other's hands and we set off at a quick pace. I resisted the urge to look over my shoulder at the growing pillar of gray smoke and ash that drifted upward. The ground tremored again as an aftershock hit. Hope whimpered in Hoot's arms.

CHAPTER 3

We made fair time descending the mountain, walking at a brisk pace when we could safely do so. Rocks, both large and small, made the going rough. We couldn't afford a twisted ankle or other injuries. While the venting of the mountain behind us hadn't worsened, it remained steady and we all feared a full eruption. Putting space between us and the danger of a pyroclastic flow was our biggest priority. Geology had been my favorite subject in high school. I knew full well that if Rainier were to erupt, the resulting river of super-heated rock, ash, and gases would destroy everything in its path.

"Looks like the snow line is ending," huffed Clark. "Off in the distance the ground is looking bare."

"We need to be on the watch for Roamers," I said quietly. "If it's thawed here, they will be too."

We kept moving, and I worried about Laura. She looked pale and I could hear a wheeze in her breathing. Hope remained with Hoot and was cuddled up to his chest sleeping soundly, secured by our makeshift sling. A cool breeze blew and the smell of burnt things hit my nose. I looked behind us to see the plume of smoke and ash drifting in our direction. The ground tremored again, knocking me off balance. I landed on my butt; pain tore through my hip. My head quickly filled with the buzzing of the dead. Hope began crying at the same time and I sensed Gus' worry. I struggled to stand as the putrid stench of the dead reached us. Hope's crying quickly turned into a high-pitched scream.

"Gus!" I yelled.

Hoot was instantly alarmed. He had spent more time amongst the dead and with me and Gus than had Clark and Laura and knew how to pick up on our subtle signals that danger was near. He positioned himself next to Gus. As I finally regained my footing, I saw the first of them. I had expected the dead to be skeletal and well decayed by the hand of time. I was sadly wrong. The creatures approaching could have been mistaken for the living. They were still far enough away that fine details were impossible to make out. Hoot clutched Hope to him, trying to calm her. She had stopped screaming but continued to cry into his chest.

"Who are they?" asked Clark.

Laura was too out of breath to say anything.

"The dead," I answered.

"Are you sure?" asked the older man. "They don't look like Roamers."

"I'm sure."

"Laura, can you take Hope?" asked Hoot quickly. "I need my arms free in order to fight."

The woman nodded and took Hope from Hoot. There were only three of the dead approaching us, but I knew there were many more not far away. My mind was overwhelmed with their signatures. I could see our small group through the eyes of the creature closest to us. It was similar to tunnel vision, as if something was blocking its peripheral vision. Like a horse with blinders on.

"There's a lot more coming behind them." My voice sounded shaky.

Gus looked at me and I knew that he was already counting in his head how many bullets we had. I knew why he was counting. Would he be able to do it? To end our lives before the Roamers could eat us alive? Could Hope possibly know that our lives were about to end, or was it strictly Gus and me who had the displeasure of that knowledge?

"Zoe, how far out are the rest?" asked Gus.

"Maybe a mile. Maybe half."

One of the Roamers raised an arm as if signaling us.

"What the fuck is it doing?" whispered Hoot.

"I swear that's a living being," said Clark. "Look at it."

"No. It's dead," I said adamantly. "The back two are Roamers. The closest one is a Runner. It wants us to think it's one of us. Alive."

Gus raised his gun, taking aim. The runner in front dropped to its knees as if surrendering. The two Roamers followed suit, landing awkwardly. They wore fresh human hides, which fell away once they were on the ground. What was underneath was beyond revolting. Their own skin had long ago liquefied and now barely coated bone. What was left behind was a layer of rot that was likely comprised mostly of bacteria and infection. I wasn't sure how any of it was still being held together. The runner in front still had bright eyes, but not the other two. Their sockets were dark voids. I refused to look into the bright eyes of the Runner, sensing that Gus was already held captive by it. I had seen the ability to mesmerize in zombie children, but not in an adult Runner before. The Runner took a position as if it were about to leap up, and smiled beneath its dead cold mask. Gus' rifle began to slump downward. No one else was making a move and even Hope's emotions were dulled within my mind. She was no longer crying.

I reached out to my husband silently and pleadingly.

Gus, you have to look away.

I got no reply. No acknowledgement whatsoever that he had "heard" me. The only thing I could sense was the Runner's rudimentary thoughts. Its reason for being here was simple: to take Hope. To destroy her. The Roamers behind it would help it kill our group while it took Hope. She was their target. The two roamers stood, and the Runner growled from deep within its core. The Roamers began to move around as if restless. My pistol was already in my hand and I aimed at the Runner. It was the one I had to kill. Not only did its thoughts of taking Hope overwhelm my mind, but so did its knowledge that Hope would have no ill effects on Runners. How the creature knew this, I wasn't sure We had assumed she could kill any of the dead.

I took aim, still avoiding the Runner's eyes, and fired. My mark was true, hitting it above the left eye.

Hope began crying again as the runner fell to the ground, finally and truly dead. The two Roamers, now free of the Runner's rule, moved hurriedly toward the rest of us.

"Shoot them!" I yelled, but was met only by Hope's cries.

I took aim and fired at the closer of the two, which still wore part of someone else's skin. Hope's high pitched screams faded into the background as the shot rang out, the expelled bullet grossly missing my target "Fuck, I missed" I screamed as the Roamer's head exploded in a mess of black gelatinous rot just. I looked to my left to see who had shot it. Laura was screaming while clutching Hope tightly to her chest. Blood ran down Laura's right arm. Wind whipped at us suddenly, battering my face with dirt and my own hair. I was so focused on Hope and the Roamer that lay in a heap at Laura's feet that the whirring thump-thump-thump from above escaped my notice until it was directly overhead. Clark lay beside his wife in two pieces. Loops of bowel stretched from his torso in a bloody trail toward his severed lower half. He was already dead. Gus and Hoot ran haphazardly toward Laura, but I got there first. I tried to pry my daughter from her arms while gunfire sounded around us.

Laura's been bit! I reached out to Gus silently, knowing he'd never hear me over the sounds of Laura and Hope both wailing and the helicopter that now hovered above.

Hope's memory of touching the roamer that killed Clark and bit Laura flashed in my own mind. Blood was smeared on the side of Hope's pale face and pooled at Laura's feet. Laura dropped to her knees, obviously weak and dying. Part of her throat was missing and her eyes bulged. She continued to clutch Hope tightly despite Gus trying to force her hands from our little girl.

I dared to look beyond our group and saw the vastness of the horde for the first time. There were hundreds of them. Roamers, Runners, Islanders, Children. Laura's grip on Hope didn't falter, even when she died and woke as one of the dead. Panic set in as her dead eyes instantly set upon our little girl. Her life as the undead was blessedly brief. Her direct contact with Hope brought her final death, not affording her the opportunity to bite our baby. Laura dropped to her side, still, and Gus was finally able to take Hope into the safety of his embrace. Wind whipped wildly against us and the noise of the helicopter hovering overhead, was deafening.

A man dressed in camo waved us toward him as the chopper landing skids touched down nearby. I looked at Gus and nodded. He approached the stranger, delivering our daughter into the arms of another man. We had no choice. Stay and die, or trust people who had appeared out of thin air.

***

Had it not been for our location being void of trees, and for the chopper that appeared, we all would have died. Hoot, Gus, myself, and Hope were the only ones to make it out. One of the helicopter crew was lost as we lifted off; a Roamer pulled him from the still-open door. It happened so fast, none of us had a chance to try to save him.

A woman pointed to a headset that hung on the bulkhead close to Hoot. He placed the device over his head and was answering the woman as she spoke to him. The sound of the chopper blades was too loud to hear what they were saying. Two men sat across from us, and one gave us a 'thumbs up' signal. I kept Hope on my lap, a lap belt tightened around both of us. I could feel my heart beating rapidly, and could sense Gus' mistrust of these new people mingled with the overwhelming sadness and horror of losing Clark and Laura. Hope rested her head on my shoulder, struggling to catch her breath through her tears. When I realized her dress was covered in Laura's still-wet blood, I wanted to vomit.

CHAPTER 4

As the pilot flew us away from the danger of the mountain, I forced myself to remain calm for the sake of our little girl. Gus and Hoot both looked absolutely haggard. The overall mood inside the helicopter was grim. Each of us had lost someone, including the crew. My sense of time was distorted by adrenaline, fear, and grief, and relief at our rescue.

I watched the ground as the chopper descended. It didn't look like much. A large field divided by a two-lane highway, the asphalt jutted and broken. Old cars dotted the road and a truck and trailer lay overturned in the field to the east of the highway. A large area of stagnant water threatened to swallow the back end of the trailer. I looked at Gus, who was as full of questions as I. Hope looked at me with her pale eyes and frowned. I couldn't help but wonder if she knew something that we didn't.

Hoot gave us a nod up as the skids touched down on the broken remains of asphalt, giving us all a bit of a jolt. The two men sitting across from us got into position at the opening on the side of the chopper and jumped down to the ground. An eerie silence fell as the motor was shut off and the blades came slowly to a rest.

"Captain, we're off to look for them. We'll check in at 1510 – if we don't we'll rendezvous back at base on foot," said the woman who sat across from Hoot.

"Rodger," said the man up front. "Setting timer for fifteen. Stay alive out there, Dayton. We can't afford to lose anyone else today."

The woman nodded grimly at him before turning to address us. "You four stay here. If we don't make it back, Harris up front will get you back to base."

She joined the other two on the ground before we could answer. I watched the group of three run toward the overturned semi.

"Hoot?" asked Gus, hoping he could clarify what was going on.

"She told me they have a secure base. They're on a survivor run right now, looking for people like us."

"She's right," said Harris from the cockpit threshold. "We've built up a fair sized city of sorts. Good people, and the most security I've come across since this all began."

"So they're going after other people?" I asked.

The pilot nodded. "Our land scouts spotted a couple of people to the east a few weeks ago. We were out trying to locate them again when the mountain started acting up. We didn't see any signs of the living here so went on to check out the volcano. It's a bit too close to our base for comfort. Good thing for you all, too. We spotted that horde and it led us to you."

"Much obliged. How far is your base?" asked Gus.

"Just south of Wenatchee. Lahar flows shouldn't reach that far, but it's still unnerving."

"How many people are they expecting to find?" I asked.

"Reports were just two adults seen. No number is too small; we aim to bring everyone in that we can. Name's Captain Harris, by the way."

"Captain, nice to meet you. Gus." I watched as Gus and the pilot shook hands. I could feel Gus' worry easing.

"This is my wife, Zoe, and our daughter Hope," he added.

Hoot stood and offered his hand. "Just call me Hoot."

Captain Harris winked at me as he shook my friend's hand. I looked away, not yet ready to trust the stranger.

"Stay alert. The dead are always nearby," said Harris. "Ma'am, I suggest you and the little one stay strapped into your seats in the event we have to take off suddenly."

Gus looked at me. "Want me to sit with her instead?"

"Yeah. I could use a quick stretch."

The truth was I felt a need to demonstrate that I wasn't some weak woman. I was, at one time, but that girl was long gone now. Gus knew me intimately through our bond, and I appreciated him offering to sit with our daughter.

Stay with her, Gus. I don't trust these people.

He leaned down and kissed me on the cheek. "I'll never leave her," he whispered. "Stay alert out there."

I will.

Hope looked at me as I stood and set her on Gus' lap. I slid down from the chopper and my feet met the old crumbling asphalt of the highway. The air was hazy from the ash that was slowly moving our direction. It smelled of earth that had been dried in the sun for too many days, stinging my nose.

I walked toward the nearest abandoned vehicle, needing a few moments to myself. The ground was uneven and the asphalt badly cracked and dotted with weeds. I focused my mind, always 'looking' for nearby dead. Sensing nothing, I walked the last few yards to a blue Porsche that had spun out long ago and sat unmoving, partially overtaken by grass and vines. Something didn't feel right. I couldn't pinpoint the cause at first, so proceeded with caution. I walked at first to the front of the car, occasionally scanning the horizon. The paint on the car was chipped and faded in places, one headlight was broken, and the tires were all flat. A box half-full of old groceries was nestled conveniently in the back seat. The canned food and a bag of chips held my attention for too long;

I almost missed the movement in the distance. It had waited for me to become distracted. I was sure of that. Somehow it had hidden itself from my mind.

Gus.

I waited for him to fill my head, hoping for some sort of reassurance. Instead, I heard shooting in the distance. I kept my eyes on the tree line. It knew I was aware of its presence. It filled my head, no longer masking itself. It was pure evil, looking to take me and my daughter. The only other time I had felt a similar signature was when the bloated eater of the dead came after Gus.

I could sense Gus in my mind, but it was overshadowed by the Hunter that was now walking my way. The creature making its way toward me appeared to be alone, and was much smaller than I had expected. It could have been a child, a dwarf, or just a very short person. It was so bloated that it was impossible to determine anything specific, like gender or age at time of death. Skin was stretched taut and translucent blue-green. As it got closer, I could see sloshing fluid beneath that awkward outer layer as the creature swayed. A breeze blew toward me, carrying with it the nauseatingly potent stench of decay mixed with rotten candy.

Gus, don't leave Hope. It was the only sensible thing I could say within my mind. It wanted both of us, and Gus had to keep our daughter safe. The only weapon I had was a hunting knife. My handgun had been lost on the mountain when I tried to remove Hope from Laura's arms.

I backed up on the road, keeping the vehicle between me and the Hunter. I could sense more of the dead now, from all directions. I could hear Gus in my head as a muddled swirl of indecision. There was little I could do, so I dropped to the ground and rolled under the vehicle. My elbows skinned on loose chunks of grit and gravel and one of my knees hit the undercarriage, sending a sharp pain jolting up my thigh. More gunfire rang out, I thought from Dayton's direction.

Gus! Get Hope out of here! My mind screamed as the Hunter's footfalls landed near my head. Its feet were covered in rotten flesh with strings of slime trailing behind. I could see foot bones as if I were staring at some macabre Halloween decoration. The transparent foot 'blob' lifted from the asphalt with a slopping sound and hands similar in texture and appearance grabbed onto the bottom edge of the car. The creature emitted a horrifying growl as it began to lift the automobile, determined to get to me. I knew instinctively that if I didn't fight, I would die. I reached for the sheath I kept secured around my right leg and pulled out my knife. As soon as I had a strong grip on it, I rolled out from under the car and toward the creature. The Hunter was clearly furious, allowing the car to drop to the ground. I stood and ran at the hideous creature, stabbing at it with full force. Intending to plant my knife into its head, the creature twisted at the last second and took my blade in its shoulder. I held onto the hilt of the knife as hard as I could, refusing to let go. The Hunter was far stronger than me, resulting in my left shoulder being pulled painfully; as it popped, my grip on the knife failed and I landed hard on my right side. I refused to cry out and did my best to roll away from the creature but met resistance when my head collided with the wrecked car. The Hunter, severely agitated, loomed over me. I could hear sloshing coming from within the beast. I was out of options, without a weapon, and without room to move. If I was going to die, I'd do as much damage as I could. I kicked upward, landing my boot as close to what should be the creature's crotch as I could figure. It remained above me, motionless. Cold fluid ran over me. I had popped it. I had actually fucking popped the bastard. I watched as the creature, almost in slow motion, deflated. Chunks fell on top of me. Some were thick liquid, some solid, some had hair, and it all smelled absolutely putrid. The Hunter stood there as its pelvic bone dropped from it and onto my foot. It was followed by a section of its spine. It was easy to see now why the creature had appeared so short; its bones had collapsed in upon themselves. Finally, the softer innards evacuated themselves from the opening my foot had created. It had turned inside out, at least partly. It lay there quivering, unable to lift its appendages. I stood, nursing my left arm, and used my boot to deliver a death blow to its head. My breath caught in my chest when one of the clumps that lay at my feet was clearly part of a small face with a section of pale white hair, now filthy. My thoughts instantly went to Hope, and I forced them out of my head.

The blades of the chopper began to spin in the distance. I looked toward it and saw someone running toward me. They were yelling, but I couldn't hear what they were saying. Hoot. It was Hoot running toward me. He was waving his arms, and instinctively I looked behind me. Roamers. So many of them. I grabbed onto my injured arm to stabilize it, and began running toward Hoot and the helicopter. The Roamers were slow and far enough away that they seemed harmless. I sensed more at play, though, and had since before the Hunter attacked me. Gus must have picked up on my concern and sent Hoot to help me. He would have stayed with Hope; of that I was certain. Gunfire rang out again, near the helicopter. I looked and saw the team had returned and were loading people onto the chopper. Two of the team of three were busy shooting at a variety of dead that were creeping out of the tree line nearest to them while the third assisted the other survivors aboard. A thunderous explosion rang out and my feet met the pavement in wobbly steps. I looked to my side in horror as a mushroom-like pillar of gray rose in the sky above Mt. Rainier.

Hoot was knocked off balance to his knees and I struggled to remain upright. The ground continued to rumble and the resulting thunderous noise was heart stopping. There was no mistaking it; Mt. Rainier was erupting. The pyroclastic flow was mesmerizing, but I knew Hoot and I had to get back to the chopper. I looked back in his direction and saw him standing again. He motioned me forward, and I ran like hell. I was only a yard away when the shock wave of the eruption hit us. I landed face down, the wind knocked out of me. Hoot screamed for me to get up and run. I used my forearms to push up off the asphalt, but dropped again when my injured shoulder gave out. Doing my best to ignore the pain wasn't working, so I got angry and used it in my favor. My next attempt brought me to my feet. The volcanic eruption was occurring to my right and a hot wind blew against me. Hoot faced the helicopter, but waited for me. His arm stretched back toward me, offering me his hand. By the time I reached him, the helicopter was lifting off. Anger boiled from within Gus and I could feel despair from Hope.

Hoot and I continued to run hoping it would hover long enough for us to make critical contact. The sky was darkening as hot ash and earth blocked the sun's rays. Bolts of lightning flashed from within the eruption. The noise from the helicopter was muted by the sounds of the earth revolting, but with each flash of lightning I could see that we were closer to our target. The chopper finally hovered above us and someone waved us back. I stepped back, pulling Hoot with me. The chopper lowered enough for us to climb onto a skid, where one of the crew helped us into the body of the bird.

"Go! Go! Go!" I heard a woman yelling.

Gus slid his arms under my own and pulled me in, away from the open side of the helicopter. The machine lurched as Harris fought to take off, the thermals from the eruption causing extreme turbulence. Between the storm around us and the rotors of the chopper it was impossible to hear anything. I could feel Hope in my head. She was scared and confused. She didn't know the person who was holding her, but it was the commotion that had her the most worried. Gus wrapped his arms around me and held me tight. I clung to him and clenched my eyes shut. The lurching of the flight made me queasy, as did the smell I had acquired when Hunter innards fell all over me.

CHAPTER 5

The chopper set down in a field next to the Colombia River. A circular area had been cleared and covered in gravel, a large "H" spray painted in white. Harris, the pilot, shut the machine down and we waited for the blades to stop spinning before speaking to us.

"There'll be time for proper introductions later. Right now we need to stay quiet and make our way to the river. We'll make our way to the base by boat."

"Why can't we just fly there?" asked a man I hadn't yet met, another survivor.

"Can't risk the dead following the chopper there," answered Dayton.

"How far is this base?" asked Gus, who was still holding me with one arm. He quietly slipped his pistol to me.

Hope was asleep on the woman's lap. She was older than me, closer to Gus in age, and had stunning Asian features. The woman was stroking our daughter's fair hair. She smiled weakly at me, and I instantly trusted her – something rare for me.

"It'll take about half an hour, assuming the trip goes smoothly," added Captain Harris.

"Stay close. Once we get to the boat we'll need to uncover it, board, and push off quickly."

"Let's go. The chopper always attracts the dead and they'll be close behind," said Harris.

"I need to stabilize Zoe's shoulder," said Gus as the others began preparing to exit the helicopter. "I think it might be dislocated".

"No, I'll be okay for now." I looked at Gus and he nodded. "The dead are near," I added.

"Okay. I want you to keep ahold of it with your right hand to support it though," he said

"I'll take Hope," offered Hoot.

"Is that her name?" asked the woman who held our daughter.

"It is," said Gus.

"I'm Autumn. This is my brother, Casper."

The man with her had been so quiet, I had all but overlooked him. He looked roughly the same age as his sister, but had a streak of gray in his long hair, which was pulled back into a man-bun. He looked up suddenly. He was muscular and his face was angular. He was clearly terrified. I knew what horrors they must have faced.

"Just call me Cas," he said in a deep voice.

"People, introductions later," said Harris. "Dead are in our sights."

"Let's go," said Hoot.

"Dayton, take the lead," ordered Harris.

We spilled out of the helicopter. Autumn handed Hope over to Hoot.

"Keep behind me," said Dayton. "The boat's just ahead about a hundred yards."

"Hill, Adams, pull up the rear. Harris and I can get the boat uncovered," said Dayton.

Dayton took off at a fair jog, and we all followed her lead. Running was painful, so I gripped my injured arm and forced myself forward. The ground was sloped slightly downward, the terrain rough. Signatures of the dead filled my head and came from all directions. My pulse beat loudly in my ears, eventually drowned out by the moans of the dead and Hope crying softly.

Gus passed me as the river came into view, following Dayton to the boat. Harris grabbed onto my good arm and pulled me after him, urging me onward. I knew already that the dead were close on our heels. By the time we reached the craft, the others had the tarp removed and were helping Autumn and Casper aboard. Gus took Hope from Hoot's arms and handed her to Dayton, who was the closest person on board. Hoot was next, followed quickly by Gus. Once Harris and I reached the small craft, I grabbed onto Gus' outstretched arm and frantically clambered aboard.

"Harris, watch out!" yelled Dayton.

I spun around to find Harris pushing us offshore. A Roamer was directly behind him. He never wavered in his duty to cast us off. He never turned to see what was behind him. He already knew; I could see it in his eyes. The creature reached him as the boat drifted just outside of his reach. Grabbing onto Harris' legs, it knocked him down. To my horror, Gus jumped into the water. He landed poorly, losing his footing in the mud and muck.

"Gus! No!" I screamed.

More of the dead were closing in. They were so close that I could smell their stink and feel their hunger deep within my mind. The hair on my arms stood on end and Hope wailed in the background. Harris was on his back, kicking at the Roamer. His screams quickly drowned out those of my daughter. As Gus neared Harris, the Roamer became agitated. Blood mixed with the murky river water, darkening it even further. I held my breath and watched as Dayton jumped overboard and joined Gus and Harris in the struggle.

I drew pistol and took aim at the Roamer. Its jerky movements and the rocking of the boat made it difficult to aim, and the chance of hitting Gus or Dayton was too risky. Harris stopped kicking at the creature and it was clear that his left leg had been mangled just above the ankle. His camo cargo pants were ripped and shreds of flesh hung in a bloody mess. The Roamer wore a crazed expression filled with hunger and lunged at Gus. Dayton grabbed Harris under the arms and dragged him farther into the water, where a man leaned over and helped hoist the injured man aboard.

Gus was trying to hold the Roamer back, and in the process lost his footing again. I soon realized that the Roamer wasn't trying to take Gus, but rather trying to get through him to the rest of us.

"Hill, we have to go!" yelled Adams. The roar of the boat motor coming to life seemed to confuse the Roamer. "Go!" repeated the man in a forceful voice.

Gus. They were going to leave Gus. I panicked, looked at Hoot and Hope, and did the unforgivable. I jumped over, leaving our daughter in the care of our dear friend. I could sense her fear and confusion, and instantly regretted my decision.

The water was deeper than I had anticipated, and I found myself fully submerged. Gus' thoughts filled my mind. His presence there provided an odd sense of comfort. He was panicked, and trying to tell me that I was in danger.

The current of the river was stronger than it appeared and surfacing seemed unlikely as I was forced toward the riverbed below. Arms that were as cold as the water wrapped around me in a death grip. I couldn't tell if they came from above or below as I continued to be battered by the current. I knew, without hesitation, that they did not belong to my husband. A searing pain ripped through my backside, just under my waistline. I assumed it was one of the jagged rocks that littered the bottom of the river. The pain in my butt grew worse. I instinctively moved my hand to where the pain was, only to meet a handful of scalp and hair. I fought the urge to inhale, knowing that if the creature that was latched onto me didn't kill me, water in my lungs would. Twisting, I fought to pry the jaws of the dead from my flesh. My hands slipped on its slime-coated flesh, my knuckles grazing what felt like teeth. I kicked where the rest of the body should be, but my feet met only the bottom of the river. Just as I made one final attempt to free myself, the pain in my butt grew so intense that my body finally took over in a desperate attempt for air. I inhaled a large volume of river water. There was a searing pain in my lungs and my eyes opened wide. My body retched, fighting the foreign substance that was now within my lungs. Silver sparkles filled my vision and soon black crept in from the edges. My body began to calm and my thoughts turned to the people whom I loved the most. Gus. Hope. My peripheral vision went dark, leaving only a narrow tunnel of light. Inside that light I saw one of the greatest loves of my life, Boggs. smiling at me. I smiled back, closed my eyes, and enjoyed a false sense of warmth as I lost consciousness.

CHAPTER 6

I didn't want to wake up. It hurt to breathe and whoever was hitting me on the chest was making me want to vomit. I wanted to yell at them to stop, but couldn't speak. I could barely breathe.

"Zoe, cough it up!" yelled Gus.

Someone forced me to roll onto my left side. Cold water flowed from my mouth and nose, and the bitterness of bile filled my throat and mouth.

"She's alive," said one of the men on board.

Hope was still crying.

"Hope," I gasped between coughing fits.

"She's fine, darlin', just breathe."

My ass hurts.

Gus rubbed at my back forcefully, and I vomited again.

I know, baby, just focus on breathing.

"Hold him down!" yelled Dayton.

Harris was screaming; the noise from the boat motor wasn't enough to drown out his cries of agony.

"Gus, we need you over here!" called Hoot.

"I can't leave her, brother," he yelled back.

"God damnit, Hills! Hold his arms down! Adams, stop the boat!" ordered Dayton.

Hope continued to wail and her fear crept into my soul, where it took an icy hold. She was telling me, without using words, that danger was near, that she was with the pretty new woman, and that she was scared for me and the man who was yelling.

"Casper, we need you!" shouted Hoot.

"Hold his leg!"

Harris screamed shrilly as the boat slowed and came to a stop. I fought against the pain in my shoulder and my butt and sat up. Gus kept me close to him for warmth. I stared in horror as four men held Harris down. He fought back despite looking like he was near death. Blood pooled at his feet. His military cargo pants had been torn off, exposing his bitten ankle. Dayton knelt beside his injured leg with a hacksaw in hand. She struggled to tie a rubber tube around his leg, just below the knee. Autumn's brother, Casper, held his leg down, pressing on his kneecap. Blood streaked Dayton's face and arm.

I quickly looked toward the bow of the boat and was glad that Autumn was holding Hope's head against her chest so that she would not see the horror that was about to happen.

Gus wrapped an arm around me and whispered into my ear. "Look away, darlin'."

"It won't help, Gus. He's already one of them," I choked out. "He's about to change."

"Fuck, they have to get away from him," he muttered as he stood.

I wanted to call out to him, but my throat hurt too bad to speak above a whisper.

"He's turning!" shouted Gus. "It's too late! Get away from him!"

The group of four men and one woman looked up, their eyes wide. Dayton tilted her head to the side, almost as if asking him if he was sure. She held the saw mid-air for a lingering moment before deciding that Gus was right. She set the saw down and stood to address the others.

"He's infected," she said as she continued to look at Gus. I assumed she meant Harris, but when Adams and Hill looked at her I understood that she meant Gus. "He says Harris is turning. Only an infected could know that. We need to end this. We owe it to Harris."

Adams, Hill, Hoot, and Casper continued to hold Harris down. He was thrashing more wildly than before and his screams were changing to something more primal. Dayton unsheathed a hunting knife from her belt, knelt again, whispered something close to Harris' ear, and promptly drove the blade into one of his eyes. The signature of the undead Harris that was inside my mind faded.

***

"You're tainted," spat Dayton with a snarl. She was looking directly at Gus.

"Zoe and I both are," he answered.

"You should have told us sooner." Hill said, angrily.

"We've been infected for a long time. We're not a danger to you," answered Gus.

"We know," said Dayton. "There's others like you back home at the base. We're trying to figure out what causes some to turn, and others, like you, don't."

"Your daughter's infected too?" asked Hill.

"We're not really sure. She's pretty special though," I said in a hoarse voice.

"What does she do?" asked Dayton. "They can all do something," she added when I didn't respond.

"They?" asked Gus.

"She's not the only one. There's three more back home. Two of them seem to be able to talk to each other without using any words and one can drop the dead to their knees when she cries. It's pretty incredible."

Gus and I looked at each other.

"She can kill them with her touch," Gus said while still looking at me. I felt my stomach drop. I didn't want them knowing too much about our little girl. What he said to only me, in my mind, worried me more.

Don't let them know you were bit.

I kept my gaze on Gus, picking up on his fear.

"We need to get moving," said Dayton in a disturbed tone.

"What about Harris?" asked Hill.

"He'd say to leave him here. You know that," said Dayton.

When Adams and Hill picked up Harris' body to throw it overboard, I looked away. The resulting splash from the body hitting the water was too much a reminder of when we said goodbye to Emilie.

"Is she okay?" asked Autumn, gesturing toward me.

"She'll be fine," said Gus. The look in his eyes was frightening me.

I watched Hope as I remained on the damp floor of the boat. I ignored my own shivering and waited to feel some sign of myself turning after being bit.

You'll be okay, darlin. I'm here.

I'm cold.

You'll be okay. He echoed his thought.

"Hoot, brother, can you find something to cover Zoe with? A tarp, or blanket?"

"There's a solar blanket in the emergency kit under the bow. Adams, can you grab it?" asked Dayton. She looked a bit sick to her stomach. "Hill, get us the fuck out of here."

Hill started the boat motor and we began moving away from the large horde that were spilling into the river.

Adams emerged from the bow, where he had ducked down to retrieve a plastic box from a small storage area under the dash. I cleared my throat and lungs again, the action sending a jolt of pain through my shoulder. Gus took the solar blanket from him and wrapped it around both of us. The boat ride lasted about twenty agonizingly long minutes. I wasn't sure how much more I could take.

Hill decreased speed near a willow tree that covered a large portion of riverbank. The surrounding landscape was barren and I thought this must be what Hell looked like. The tree was grossly out of place and made for an excellent land mark.

"We're here," announced Dayton coldly as the boat glided ashore.

"Stay quiet. The Deadheads will be coming soon. They can sense infected like you, and we can't afford to lose any more time. We need to get to base by dark. Do what you need to keep the little one quiet, too," instructed Hill.

I looked to the west and realized the sun was low in the sky. Night would be upon us soon.

"Hoot, I need you to carry Hope," said Gus.

"Sure," he answered without hesitation. "C'mon, sweetie," he said in his best 'your uncle loves you' voice. She reached out to him and appeared glad to be back in familiar arms. "You have to stay very quiet, princess, okay?"

She nodded and put one of her pudgy little fingers up to her mouth. Hoot smiled sweetly at this gesture.

"We'll need to travel by foot for about two miles," said Hill quietly. "There's not much between here and there for cover, so be fast and stay quiet."

"Rodger that," said Gus.

Zoe, I need you to stand up and keep your butt turned away from everyone while I wrap the blanket around you.

I looked at Gus with knowing eyes. He held a hand out for me, which I gratefully held onto with my non-injured arm. I hoisted myself up, pain ripping through both my shoulder and my butt cheek. He wrapped the thin thermal sheet tightly around me and we waited for the others to step off the boat. No one had taken notice of my rear end since I had remained seated. Dayton waited onboard, and I knew then that she intended to be that last one to disembark.

She started at us as if waiting, but neither of us moved. She lowered her gaze to the floor of the boat where we had been huddled together for warmth. She adjusted her stance and her face took on a look of anger.

"What's the blood from?" she demanded.

I felt the warmth leave my face.

"Nothing to worry about," answered Gus.

"Like hell it's not," said Dayton.

Hoot stood on shore with Hope and I could tell he sensed that we were in danger by the look on his face.

Autumn and Casper stood back a few feet, clearly confused. Hill and Adams took defensive postures.

"She's fine," said Gus in a deepened voice.

"Is she bit?" demanded Dayton. Gus didn't answer. "*Is she bit*?" she yelled this time.

"She's already infected, and I'd know if she were turning," he answered. His voice was almost feral and made my blood run cold.

"Fuck no, we can't take that risk. No fucking way almighty," said Dayton as she shook her head back and forth. "She stays behind. Period."

"Then I stay with her."

Hoot stepped sideways, away from the others, with Hope still in his arms.

"And we stay with them," our friend quickly interjected.

"No," I said angrily. "It's not safe out here for Hope."

"Zoe, we can't just leave you here."

I looked at Gus in desperation. *You have to take her, Gus. You have to go with her and keep her safe.*

"We can leave you with a day's worth of water and your weapons," said Dayton, still not backing down.

Gus cleared his throat.

"Give us twenty-four hours. Tell us where your base is and if we make it there un-turned, will you let us in?"

Dayton looked at her companions before looking back at us. "Forty-eight, and not sooner. And that's if the others back home agree."

"Done. Hoot, take Hope and go with them," said Gus.

I looked at him angrily. "No, Gus! You have to go with her!"

He looked down at me. "I will not leave you out here alone, darlin'. Never. Hoot will watch over her like she's his own and you know that."

I was too angry, and too out of ideas, to argue.

"Let me hold her before you leave," I demanded.

"No. We can't risk her getting hurt," said Dayton, which infuriated me.

"Zoe, it's okay. We'll see her in two days," Gus said, trying to calm me.

I looked at Hoot. "You promise you'll watch after her? With your life?"

He nodded.

Hill took a small spiral bound notebook from his right vest chest pocket, a pen from the left pocket, and scribbled a map. He set it on a bow seat and backed away.

Dayton went ashore and joined the others, leaving me and Gus in the half-beached boat. Hill secured one end of a rope to the willow tree and I watched as my heart was carried away. I took a deep shuddering breath, trying my hardest to not break down.

"Darlin', we'll get there. I promise."

I turned around to face my husband, letting the solar blanket fall from me. I slapped Gus on his chest with my good hand, as hard as I could.

"Why! Why'd you let them take her?" I shouted. "She's gone!"

He allowed me to slap his chest two more times before grabbing my arm, stilling me.

"It was the only way, Zo. Something about Adams told me to let it go. I couldn't read his mind, nor he ours, but I sensed something. He's infected too, I'm sure of it, and while Dayton appeared to be in charge, she wasn't. That man was ready to kill you, Zoe."

"You should have let him!" I spat angrily. "You should be with Hope now, not here with me!"

"I made a promise to someone a long time ago, to keep you safe, and I plan to honor my word. You're half of me, woman. Half of me, and the most important and the best half."

He wrapped his arms around me and held me close, despite my protesting.

"Zoe, we need to move. We have to find shelter for the night. Not only are the dead going to follow us, but we need to get inside and out of whatever fallout there's going to be from the mountain."

"Just leave me behind," I mumbled into his chest. My muscles relaxed as I finally allowed him to hold me.

"Stop talking like that. Hope needs you, and so do I. Are you going to be able to walk?"

"Do I have a choice?"

"No."

"Then yes. I can walk."

"Take your pants off. I need to check that bite. They left the first aid kit, so I'll clean and bandage it real quick. Then we need to get the fuck out of here."

"Okay."

I gently pushed away from him and slipped out of my jeans. I pulled my panties down and turned my backside to my husband.

"Does it hurt?' he asked.

"Like a mother," I grumbled.

"It got you pretty good. Lean over the back of the driver's seat. This might sting."

I took a painful step forward and leaned over the seat-back.

"Try to hold still, darlin'. That bastard got you pretty good. I know you heal fast but you're still bleeding, so stitches may be a good idea. Hopefully this first aid kit has some."

"Great," I replied. "That's gonna hurt."

"Ayup."

Gus began rifling through the first aid kit noisily. The dead began filling my head again and my bite and hip throbbed.

"I found a pack of sutures but no needles," grumbled Gus.

"They're getting closer," I said.

"Yeah, I know. Take a deep breath, babe."

I inhaled deeply and waited for whatever he was about to do. I felt something cold run down the back of my leg the same time that my wound began stinging.

"What the hell was that?" I asked through clenched teeth.

"Rubbing alcohol. To disinfect it."

"God, that hurt like a son of a bitch!" I groaned through clenched teeth.

"Sorry. I had to."

"I know. Just hurry and finish?"

"Hold still. I'm going to dry it off with a sterile gauze and bandage it. Hopefully that'll be enough to slow the bleeding."

It took Gus only a minute to slap a dressing on. It took him another minute to fashion a sling for my arm using an ACE wrap. Once he was done I leaned over the side of the boat and rinsed my panties out using the river water. They were badly stained with my blood. I wrung them out the best I could while using just one arm and slid them back on, but didn't bother with my jeans. Gus folded the solar blanket into a small rectangle and shoved it into the pocket of his still-damp cargo pants. I quickly put my wet socks and shoes back on.

"How far off do they feel?" he asked me.

"Maybe half a mile."

"Let's get out of here then."

I nodded.

"You going to be okay without pants?"

"I'll manage," I answered quickly.

The sun was low in the horizon and burning a bright red.

"The smoke's working its way this direction," I said.

"Yeah. You can tell it's polluting the horizon. Out through the bow, babe."

I followed him to the open bow. He picked up the paper that Hill left behind. He unfolded it and studied it before pointing to the west.

"Map says to head that way. He marked two X's, so I'm hoping the closest is shelter."

"Let's go."

My heart ached for my daughter. The pain of being separated from her was far worse than that of my shoulder, hip, or butt bite. We set off to the west, trying to keep ahead of the dead that followed.

CHAPTER 7

As the sun began to drop, so did the temperature. Our clothes were still damp from the river and while my injuries made walking difficult, I knew we had to keep moving to stay warm.

"Any idea how far the nearest city is?" I asked.

"Hoping very far away, darlin'."

"But we need to get inside."

"Ayup. But cities mean hordes. Hoping we come across a road soon, maybe find a remote house."

Still no signs of old civilization, our pace quickened. Our shadows grew long in front of us. Gus took hold of my hand when I began to slow. My muscles burned from the exertion of walking after already being exhausted from my ordeal in the river. We walked another mile before finally happening upon a two-lane highway. Like most roads since the end of the world, it was littered with weeds and old trash. A few wrecked cars and an old pickup truck were left abandoned on the side of the road. A deer carcass lay in a heap not far from where we crossed, badly decayed, with bones from its limbs spread randomly nearby. The hide was shredded and tufts of fur remained in a few select patches.

"Fucking Roamers," grumbled Gus.

"Yeah," I said in agreeance.

I was out of breath and ready to stop. Sensing my weariness, Gus slowed our pace but kept hold of my hand.

***

We followed the curve of the highway to our right, always alert to the threat of the dead. Ash began to lazily fall from the sky. Gus silently told me to breathe through my nose to best filter the substance.

There. I pointed.

I see it.

In the distance, pink light from the setting sun reflected brightly, offering hope of respite. Gus squeezed my hand and looked at me intently.

You ready?

I nodded. I mustered together my remaining energy and we sprinted forward, desperate to find lodging.

The Columbia River loomed before us. A metal-and-concrete bridge with two lanes each direction was a welcome sight. At the far end, a stone tower stood as a beacon of hope. The dead surrounded us in the distance. While we couldn't see them, my mind told me they were there.

"We don't have much time. They're getting closer," I said quietly as we stopped long enough to decide which approach to the tower would be best.

"We'll need to climb down the ridge, darlin'. It'll be faster than following the bend in the road."

The side of the highway dropped off by several yards. We straddled the metal barrier at the road's edge and began to scale our way down the slope toward the bridge. The soil was dry and rocky, making for loose footing. I fell several times, and as painful as each landing was I refused to cry out. I could feel the dead close behind and I knew any extra noise would only hasten their approach. We reached the bottom of the drop-off as the moans of Roamers became audible. Out of breath and exhausted, I kept hold of Gus' hand for dear life. We jogged until we got back to the highway. My old hip wound began to ache, signaling the dead were getting closer. As we reached the barrier alongside the road, Gus quickly lifted me over, back onto the highway.

"We have to get inside," I said. "They're so close."

"I can smell them," he answered.

The moans of the dead were unnerving to say the least. Some sounded like dying cattle while others sounded like choking pigs. My stomach lurched in protest at the stench of decaying flesh. I looked behind us. Oddly, I didn't sense or see anything but slow Roamers; about a dozen or so. They were usually accompanied by at least one or two of the faster Runners. Fear ran through me that we were not running from them, but rather being herded.

Don't try to guess, Darlin'. Just keep moving.

Gus squeezed my hand and I eagerly returned the gesture. We advanced on the roadway, focused on the tower that stood on the other side of the bridge. No longer caring about making noise, our footfalls upon asphalt grew heavy as we sprinted the last hundred yards or so. The road was in rough shape with many cracks and potholes. A gust of wind swept by, bringing with it the smell of ash and soot.

"Zoe, as soon as we get there we'll try the door first. If it's locked I want you to climb the metal ladder that's going up the side. I'll be right behind you."

I didn't answer, focusing my energy on reaching the structure.

As we reached the tower door, it suddenly opened inward.

"Quick, get inside," came a deep male voice.

We paused for a brief moment, knowing that no one was to be trusted.

"Unless you want those bastards to eat you, *get inside*," repeated the man.

I pulled on Gus' hand, urging him to accept the invitation. We quickly rushed inside and were met with darkness. The door slammed shut and the moans from the dead instantly quieted. The sound of the locks on the door engaging brought much needed comfort. The stranger struck a match and the light from the flame danced around the room in which we stood.

"No idea who you people are, but the Deads will be here knocking in about sixty seconds. If you can help shoot we can knock 'em all out within a couple minutes. Guns are up top," he said as he lit a candle and set it on a small table.

"Show me where," said Gus.

The man nodded and quickly began climbing a narrow metal ladder that led to a loft. Gus followed.

"Zoe, stay down there so you don't hurt your arm," Gus called back to me.

They quickly reached the loft and their voices carried down to where I waited.

***

"I assume you know how to shoot?"

"Ayup."

"Goes without saying, but get the closest ones first."

"Ayup."

Their awkward discussion was interrupted by gunfire as they shot the advancing Roamers. Ignoring Gus' instructions to remain below, I climbed the ladder one-handed. As I scaled the rungs, each resulting jolt of my body sent a sharp pain through my shoulder.

"That's all of them," said Gus.

"We need to dump the bodies over the bridge rail or they may attract unwanted guests. Name's Sam, by the way. Let's get to work."

"I'm Gus."

I cleared my throat as I pulled myself onto the floor of the loft.

"I'm Zoe."

"Zo, you were supposed to stay down there."

I rolled my eyes at my husband, irritated by how he was treating me like a child.

Are you injured?" Sam addressed me.

"Yeah. She banged up her shoulder and I need to patch up her backside. I'll tell you right now she's been bit."

"Crap," said the man. "Any signs of turning?"

"None. She and I are both infected. Have been for a while. She won't turn."

"That seems to be the way it goes. My brother's infected and got the shit torn out of his arm. I watched him like a hawk for almost a week before I finally realized he wasn't gonna turn into one of those bastards. We'll get rid of the Deads then she can get cleaned up.

"We're headed out to clear bodies," said Gus.

"I heard. I can help."

"Not with your shoulder," said Gus.

Sam looked at me and winked. "He's right. You can't afford to be broke any more than you are. We won't be long. There's clean water in gallon containers downstairs. Feel free to use the wash basin on the table. Only drink from the 1-liter plastic bottles, though. The other water hasn't been boiled."

"Thanks," I said.

"Darlin', I'll check and re-bandage that bite as soon as we get back inside."

"Okay, but I don't like you going out without me."

"You'll want this," said Sam as he handed Gus a strap-on head-lamp to wear. "Miss, there's more candles downstairs on the table. Feel free to light them if you need to. The way the loft is constructed, the light won't reach up here. We keep it dark so we're not noticed."

"Thanks."

"Okay, let's do this," said Gus.

The three of us took turns climbing back down the ladder and I watched as they opened the door and stepped out into the night air. Bodies in various stages of decay littered the bridge deck. Sam handed Gus a pair of thick work gloves and the two of them began lifting bodies and tossing them over the rail and into the river below. I left the door open and walked to the small bistro table that sat off to one side. It became increasingly hard to see as the dark of night laid its claim on the tower. The candles were where Sam said they'd be, but I opted to not waste resources by lighting a second. Shadows danced on the walls in eerie patterns. The footprint of the stone tower was small, perhaps the size of a child's bedroom. A stash of water sat along the bottom of one section of wall, in both gallon and 1-liter sizes. Four cardboard boxes were stacked next to the water supply, labeled "MREs."

The only furniture in the space consisted of the bistro table, an overstuffed easy chair and small ottoman, and two plastic patio chairs. I helped myself to a 1-liter of water and guzzled it quickly. I hadn't realized my throat was dry. As badly as I wanted to sit, my backside hurt too much to do so comfortably. I used my good arm to gingerly remove the ace-wrap-sling that Gus fashioned back on the boat. My shoulder was stiff, but not hurting as badly as before. I attributed that to my being infected and my resulting accelerated healing. I moved it slowly, trying to get back some range of motion. I was still damp from my dunk in the river, so peeled off my remaining clothes and grabbed an afghan that I found on the back of the easy chair. The tower wasn't roomy and I grew claustrophobic quickly. I wrapped myself in the afghan and once again climbed the metal ladder to the loft. The loft floor was metal and covered only two-thirds of the floor below. Safety railing extended the length of the open side, save for a small opening where the ladder met the floor. Windows stood knee-level to about six feet up the wall, lining every other angled wall. A mattress and sleeping bag sat on the floor to my left. A simple home-made wooden gun rack stood between two of the eight windows. Two rifles remained, along with several boxes of ammo. The remainder of the space was empty.

Exhausted, I made my way to the mattress and allowed myself to lay down. It wasn't the most comfortable and smelled strongly of must, but was by far better than the hard floor. I closed my eyes and pictured Hope in my mind. I refused to think of her scared, or alone, or worried about us. Instead, I pictured her on a sunny day running through a mountain meadow.

***

I woke to the sound of Gus and Sam talking. I was surrounded by darkness and it took a moment for my eyes to adjust.

"Gus?" I called out.

"I'm down below, darlin'. I'll be right up."

His voice was reassuring. I knew where I was, but I had fallen asleep and woke disoriented.

Sam's voice carried. "Go ahead and turn in for the rest of the night. I'll keep watch and Hans should be here at first light."

"Wake me up if there's any trouble," replied Gus.

He made a bit of a racket climbing the ladder as his boots fell heavily on each rung. The loft remained dark aside from a very faint glow from the candles burning below.

"Sorry I can't turn a light on, love. The windows up here stay uncovered at all times."

"It's okay."

"How are you feeling?" he asked me.

I quickly, and carefully, tested my shoulder and found it to be stiff but much less painful.

"Shoulder's stiff but better," I offered.

"How's your butt cheek?"

I moved my hips and found the wound to be tolerable. It felt odd, though, so I tested it with my hand.

"I bandaged it while you were asleep. It's already healing well, so no need to suture after all."

"It's not as painful."

"Good."

"Who's Hans?"

"Sam's watch partner. They take turns here. Four days on, four days off. Hans is relieving him in the morning."

"Are they with the group that has Hope?"

"Yeah. He knew enough about them to know it's the same group. Dayton's hooked up with his brother, Sam says he'll take us with him to their camp."

I sat up, excited by the news. "It hasn't been forty-eight hours yet."

"He says it will be. It's a bit of a trek. Lay down and try to get a little more sleep, Zoe. It'll be light soon."

CHAPTER 8

Morning came, and along with it a sense of both excitement and dread. Gus quietly nudged me awake and I already knew he wanted me to stay quiet, but he confirmed it by placing his index finger to his lips. Our eyes met and I listened. He filled my mind with his own worry, and I desperately tried to clear my head in order to "search" for any dead that might be nearby. There was nothing but Gus. I sat up, glad to find relief in pain from both of my injuries. Gus kept a hand on my arm and tapped his ear with his other, telling me to keep listening. I nodded in understanding.

A single small metallic tap. Then nothing but our shallow breathing. *Tap*. I looked toward the top of the ladder and cocked my head to one side. *Tap*.

"What is it?" I whispered, nearly inaudibly.

Before he could answer, something below us crashed to the floor.

"Damnit," grumbled Sam.

"Sam? Everything okay?" Gus called down.

"Yeah. Sorry if I woke you. I'm just trying to fix the door on the wood stove."

"I'll head down and lend you a hand."

"Thanks," Sam called back.

I pulled the blanket back and sat up. The room was cold and I was still nude.

Gus looked at me with longing. "I can stay up here for a few minutes," he said, his voice a bit distant.

I simply shook my head side to side. A romp in a cold loft while our daughter was somewhere unknown to us was the last thing I wanted to do.

"Can you bring my clothes up, though?"

He winked at me and proceeded to lower himself over the edge and onto the ladder. I stood and wrapped myself in the blanket to keep warm. I walked to the window. The sky was dark, heavy with clouds and ash. Volcanic debris fell from the sky lazily, resembling dirty snowflakes. We had hoped the volcanic fallout would travel a path away from us, but instead it remained a menacing shadow. A layer of gray covered the ground. The river below was murky from debris. Swirls of ash laced the river's edges where small eddies churned. A tree had fallen into the river, its branches creating a trap for anything that might float by. A dead bird had fallen victim to the tree, bobbing gently in the current. My breath caused a layer of fog to form on the pane of glass in front of me. I raised my right index finger and drew a heart for my Hope.

"Zo? I brought some clothes up for you. Your shirt and panties were dry, but your socks are still damp. Sam had these hospital scrub pants that should fit you."

I turned to face my husband. "Thanks."

"Whatcha lookin' at?"

"The ash."

"Yeah I saw that too."

"It's going to make our trip longer, isn't it?"

I heard him sigh. "Sam says their community is only about a day's walk from here. As long as it doesn't get much worse I think we'll be okay. We'll need to cover our mouths, though. We don't have masks, but can use cloth. Just something to keep the ash and soot out of our lungs."

I slipped into my underclothes while he spoke.

"When will we leave?" I asked.

"Hans is due here this morning. Sam said he'll be ready to leave within an hour of that."

"Gus?"

"Hmm?"

"Do you think we can trust him?" I asked, keeping my voice low as to not be heard by Sam.

"I think so, darlin'. I got a bad vibe from Adams but no one else so far. We'll figure it out once we're back with Hope."

Hearing her name spoken out loud made my heart sink. Gus wrapped his arms around me and I melted into him. I refused to cry. We'd need all of our energy to get to Hope and I wouldn't waste any on tears.

***

Hans' arrival was welcomed by us all, but Sam especially. The new man didn't seem surprised by our presence.

"I brought breakfast," said Hans with a smile. "We all hoped you'd end up here since it's on the way to camp. I brought a few potatoes, seven eggs, and some ketchup and parmesan cheese. Hopefully the ash hasn't gotten into my backpack and ruined any of it."

"You've seen our daughter? And our friend Hoot?" I asked.

"Yes, ma'am. They're well. I'll fill you in while Sam cooks breakfast."

Hans' coat and shoes were caked with volcanic fallout. He put his canvas backpack on the small table, causing a cloud of dust to envelope the pack.

"Hans, get out of those damned clothes before that crap gets all over," said Sam.

Hans was an older man and chuckled at Sam's command. He obliged, though, by removing his coat, shoes, and pants.

"Gus, Zoe, we'll start out right after breakfast. It'll give Hans a chance to update us on road conditions."

"Sounds good," said Gus.

The three of us sat at the small bistro table.

"First," he began, "Hope is a sweet little thing."

I smiled. "Thank you."

"She's taken to the other children really easily. They're like her…" He paused. "…from parents like you. Infected. She's been with the other kids most of the time she's been in camp. If not them, then Hoot or the new woman that came with them. Autumn."

"So she's safe, and healthy?" asked Gus.

Hans smiled. "Very. There's a dog in the compound that she's become fond of, too. A little mutt named Flower. That dog follows your little girl everywhere."

Gus chuckled.

"Anyway, Hoot wanted me to let you know that Hope's okay. She misses you, but as long as he tells her you'll be there soon she seems okay with things."

I sighed in relief.

The smell of frying potatoes filled the room.

"Hans, are these from our chickens?" asked Sam, holding up one of the eggs.

"Four of them are. The other three are from a duck clutch I came across on the way here. I just wish I could have gotten an actual duck."

"Eggs are great," I said. "Thank you."

Hans nodded at me. "You're welcome. The roads are getting pretty messy. The ash is a fine powder for the most part; we're far enough from the mountain that larger debris should be southwest of here. You should have a pretty easy trek home today, as long as you tie a bandana around your mouth and nose."

I was nearly drooling by the time the eggs hit the skillet and filled the room with their aroma.

"How's the Dead count?" asked Sam as he stirred and scraped at the eggs.

"A bit higher than usual. They're Rotters, though. Slow as hell and sloppy. They shouldn't give you too much trouble."

I looked at Gus and smiled. I could sense that he was as anxious to get going as I was.

"We had a horde here last night," said Gus while still looking into my eyes. "They followed us from the river."

"Bastards," mumbled Hans.

***

We ate breakfast quietly. The food was warm and bland due to lack of spices, but we welcomed it eagerly. The ketchup supply was meager, so I only used one of the few small packets that Hans brought with him. I didn't skimp on my portion of the food, eating just as much as any of the men.

Once we finished, Sam and Hans helped us fashion bandanas out of an old t-shirt. I used a knife to cut the bottom of it into strips, which we tied snugly over our mouths and noses. The material was thin, making breathing easier than it might have been otherwise. I used the top of the t-shirt to fashion something to protect my head and face. Hans insisted that I wear his bulky coat, since he'd be staying behind. Standing just outside the structure, I slipped into it. Ash continued to fall, quickly dusting our clothing. Gus and Sam each had a rifle slung over a shoulder. Sam wore camo cargo pants that were heavy with ammo tucked into the pockets. I opted to stick to one hand gun and a hammer. To allow both men to fight the dead without a burden on their backs, I took the only back pack, which was heavy with bottled water and basic supplies. I still nursed my shoulder, so wouldn't be of much use if we faced the dead. I tugged on the edge of my makeshift head scarf, pulling it closer to my eyes for protection. We set out single file, crossing the remainder of the bridge. Our footfalls fell quietly on the layer of ash. Tendrils of powder drifted up each time we stepped. It was disconcerting leaving tracks, but we were left with little choice. The world surrounded us in a blanket of silence aside from the lull of the flowing river below.

***

Ash obscured our view of the sky, making it impossible to track the passage of time. Our first footfalls turned into hundreds, and then thousands. There was a profound lack of dead as we continued, which made us all nervous. Hans had reported higher numbers. We walked for hours on high alert, which in itself was draining. By the time we came to the first signs that civilization had ever graced the land around us, the ambient lighting was already fading.

"Is it getting dark?" I asked.

"Either that or the smoke from Rainier is getting worse," answered Sam. "See the building up on the left? That's a hardware store. Windows are all broken out and it's been emptied. Another half-mile and we'll stop at an old farm house we have set up as a safe house."

"How much farther is your camp?" asked Gus.

"A couple hours."

"We could be there tonight," I said with excitement.

"No. We'll hole up at the farmhouse for the night, darlin'," said Gus. "Safest to be off the road after dark."

I sighed, but knew he was right. We continued on in silence. Once we passed the hardware store, I broke the silence.

"Where do you suppose they all are?" I asked.

"The dead?" asked Sam, looking for clarification.

"Yeah."

"I'm not sure, but it's making me nervous as shit," he answered.

***

As darkness grew around us, we finally came upon the farmhouse. It looked like an ancient structure. The front porch had been screened-in at some point in time, but the old metal screens were rusted through and hung in ragged shambles. The screen door was in even worse shape, hanging by an old hinge, the frame twisted backward. The wooden planks of the porch floor were covered in ash dust, but not as heavily as outside. I figured it must have blown in with the wind. A threadbare sofa sat against the far wall and piles of old junk took up each corner: a doll with no head, an ancient tricycle with a flat tire, books, and an old metal wash basin half full of soil and old weeds.

Sam lifted the wash basin and pulled out a key. A bird of prey screamed in the distance. I shivered. We entered the old house, losing the small amount of light we had left from the setting sun.

"It's safe to turn on the flashlights," said Sam. "The windows are all boarded."

Gus thoughtfully took the pack from my back. The relief was instant. The weight of the straps had begun to make my injured shoulder ache. He found one of the flashlights and quickly turned it on. The inside of the home was as aged as the porch. Furniture was sparse: a claw-foot sofa with a brown-and-orange crocheted afghan hung across its back, an old oval rag rug, and a faded green recliner in one corner. A small dog bed sat near the foot of the recliner. Lace curtains still hung in front of the only window in the room. I walked to the window and pushed the curtain aside. The glass pane remained, but like Sam had said the window was boarded over from the other side.

"Zoe?" Gus called my name.

I turned to look at him.

"Do you sense anything?"

I shook my head side-to-side. "Nothing."

"In the back of the house there's two bedrooms. Just pick one and get some rest while I take watch for a few hours," suggested Sam. "The hallway's off the kitchen. You can't miss it."

"Thanks, brother," said Gus.

"Sam? Is there any food stashed here? I'm starving," I said.

Sam was crouched near the floor, sorting through my backpack. He looked up and smiled at me. "Yup. Kitchen's just the next room over. Help yourselves."

"Thanks. I'll bring you something before we crash," I offered.

He winked at me.

I turned and followed Gus across the threshold to the next room. He set the flashlight on the only countertop in the room. The beam danced across an old lath wall with peeling plaster and wallpaper. A faded calendar from 1972 still hung on the wall. Next to the calendar hung a pale blue needlepoint that read *home is where the heart is.* An old fashioned wood-burning oven and stovetop took up half the length of another wall, and next to it sat a small square table. Another rag rug rested in the middle of the floor.

"I'll check the cabinets," I said quietly.

"Sounds good, darlin'. I'll go through some of the boxes over here."

I hadn't noticed the cardboard boxes stacked against the wall, underneath the cloth calendar. My stomach growled with hunger as I opened the first set of cabinet doors. I was surprised to see a variety of canned vegetables neatly stacked. I picked a can of sliced carrots to share with Gus. The next cabinet held single-serve packets of cherry Kool-Aid and bottled water. I opted for two bottles of plain water and skipped the flavoring. While it'd be a nice treat, the supplies didn't belong to us.

"Ahhh, look here!" said Gus cheerfully.

I looked over and saw him grinning back at me. He held out a package of Ritz crackers.

"That's not all. There's peanut butter too."

"I found canned carrots, but maybe we can save those for breakfast," I said.

"Sounds good. Let's look for a spreader knife and take these in to share with Sam."

Before long, Gus found a butter knife in a drawer and we headed back to the entry room.

While snacking on peanut butter and crackers, we talked about our plan for the next day. Sam told us the compound was only about a two hour walk from the farmhouse. We'd pack enough water and ammo to make the trek.

I yawned, exhausted from the long day of walking.

"I think I'll head to bed," I announced.

Sam stood and stretched, and Gus followed suit.

"Sam, are you sure you're up to first watch?" asked Gus.

"Yeah. It'll give me a chance to organize more weapons. We keep a stash of guns and knives under the floorboards in the kitchen. Just lift the rug and there's a metal ring to pull on. You should both check it out. This house may not look like much, but we have it pretty well fortified and stocked for emergencies. Everyone at camp knows it's here if they need it."

"Okay but holler if you need help or if trouble comes a-knockin', brother."

"Will do."

"Night," I said sleepily.

Gus wrapped an arm around me and we returned to the kitchen. The back wall connected to a hallway, the only way to go. I held the flashlight as we continued to the back of the house where Sam said the bedrooms would be.

We walked into the closest bedroom and I was glad to see an old iron-framed bed that was neatly made. A small round table sat on one side of the headboard, covered in an eyelet cloth. An old oil lamp and a Bible sat on top, but nothing else. The room was small and the only other piece of furniture, a tall-boy dresser, barely fit into the far corner of the room.

"We should check the dresser for clothes," said Gus as he yawned. Both of us could use new things that aren't falling apart."

"When we wake up. I just need to lay down and sleep."

We both stripped ourselves of our weapons. Gus set his on the dresser and I set mine on the bedside table. Even though the room was cold and I was shivering, I slipped out of my clothes and down to my under things. The thought of wearing the dirtied clothes in bed, ash and all, was not appealing.

"I should check your butt cheek, darlin'. How's it feeling?"

"It barely hurts anymore. I think it's okay. It's my shoulder that's still kinda stiff."

He walked behind me and inched my panties down just far enough to look at my bite wound. My skin felt like it was on fire when he peeled the dressing off.

"It's closed up. Just a touch of scabbing and a hint of green like your hip. Looks good. Want me to rub your neck?"

"As long as you're careful with my shoulder, that'd be great."

He took my hand and led me to the bed. He sat first, the bed frame protesting with a loud squeak. He scooched back and I sat in front of him, creating another squeak of the old-style springs beneath the mattress. I closed my eyes and Gus began kneading the flesh of my neck and shoulders.

"We'll see her tomorrow," he whispered into my left ear.

I hung my head and sighed softly. "Tomorrow," I whispered back.

He stopped massaging, allowed one arm to drape over me while he placed the other around my side. I held onto the arm that was draped over my chest and we sat like that for a long moment, in a quiet embrace. His inner thoughts touched my own and our sadness over being apart from Hope mingled together. Eventually we both crawled under the covers. We wrapped ourselves around each other for warmth and quickly fell asleep.

CHAPTER 9

"Morning, Sunshine," said Gus as I rolled over in the bed to face him.

I blinked my eyes, which were dry. "Hey."

Gus had lit the oil lamp beside the bed, making it still feel like night time. With the windows boarded, it very well might have been.

"I need to go relieve Sam and take watch. Do you want to keep sleeping?"

I shook my head side-to-side. "I'll get up with you. What time is it?"

"About two o'clock, still the middle of the night."

I groaned.

He leaned down and kissed me on the neck. His kiss was hot against my skin and his several-day-shadow was surprisingly soft. He cupped one of my breasts in his hand and began exploring my flesh with the other. As badly as my body wanted to give in and enjoy his touch, my longing for Hope was stronger.

Sensing my hesitation, he stopped and looked into my eyes. No words needed to be said aloud. He knew instantly why I was unsettled. He simply nodded, kissed me sweetly on the lips, and rolled out of bed.

I hesitantly climbed out from under the covers, the cold making me instantly regret doing so. I walked to the dresser and opened the top drawer, which was heavy and filled with ammunition. "Christ," I mumbled.

"What is it?"

"Bullets. A lot of them."

He approached to see for himself.

"Fuck. That's a lot of ammo."

He pushed the heavy drawer back in and opened the next one down.

"Holy shit," I said under my breath.

Inside the second drawer sat padded trays that looked similar to egg cartons, filled with grenades. Gus whistled inward.

"Looks like we came across the right group of people."

"I hope so. The last few haven't turned out so well."

The next three drawers were much more benign, offering us exactly what we needed - fresh clothing. They smelled musty but were clean and dry. I found a pair of low-rise jeans that were a size too large so I used the drawstring from a pair of men's exercise shorts as a belt. A purple v-neck t-shirt with a print of an old fashioned Mickey Mouse was the next best fitting thing I found, but it too was baggy on me. Gus was out of luck as everything but a pair of socks was too small for him. He pulled out a dark green hoodie and tossed it to me. I slipped it over my head and was glad for the warmth it would provide. The only socks were men's, also too large for me, but once I pulled them up to my knees I managed to get my tennis shoes on and thought about how badly I was in need of a new pair of shoes.

"We'll get you some the next time we come across 'em," said Gus as he snuffed out the wick of the oil lamp.

I smiled at him and we left the little bedroom together.

As soon as we were in the hallway and before I shut the door, Gus called out to Sam.

"Coming out."

"Great," he called back. "Come on into the dining room."

We followed the dim glow from Sam's lantern, turning the corner to the right. He was sitting at a small desk, cleaning a handgun.

"You can go sleep," I said to Sam.

"Thanks guys. Let me just finish with this gun. The window to my right has a peep door. The glass is broken out, so try to keep it shut as much as you can. Keep an eye on the weather though. Looks like a storm is brewing."

"Any issues while we slept?" asked Gus.

"Nah. Just some wind every now and then. And more ash. It's the damnedest thing. We almost always have at least a few of the Dead wander through here. But it's just…wind and ash. No signs of the Deads."

"Okay, brother. Go get some sleep."

Sam punched the clip into the pistol and stood. He left it on the desk, I assumed in case we needed it during the night.

"Sleep well," I called out as he walked down the hallway.

He raised his hand and waved acknowledgement without looking back.

"Let's settle in for a bit. Talk about our next steps."

Wind howled outside, knocking something into the side of the house.

"What if the weather's too bad to travel?" I asked, already knowing the answer.

"We have to trust that Hoot's taking care of her."

The sound of thunder cracked in the distance, shaking the old farmhouse. Once it settled, a deep quiet fell around us. We walked together into the living room and sat on an old gray velveteen sofa. The cushions sagged and the backrest was too firm, but it felt good to be close to Gus. He wrapped a hand around mine and I leaned into him. The little house groaned and creaked as another gust of wind wrapped itself around the structure. A chill crawled up my spine; before it got to the nape of my neck Gus' hand tightened around mine. I suddenly doubled over from intense and excruciating pain in my hip and abdomen. While I wanted to scream, intolerable buzzing in my head made it impossible. My eyes clenched shut and the world fell away from me. I was aware that Gus stood. Once he let go of my hand I was surrounded by darkness, hunger, and pain. Not just my own pain, but *their* pain as well. Their darkness. Their insatiable hunger. I could hear Gus and Sam talking loudly, but wasn't sure what they were saying. There was another noise drowning their words, like a TV channel blaring static. Gus was trying to get into my head, and I fought hard to fight my way out of the virtual pit of despair that the dead created.

"Zoe, they're surrounding the house. Do they know we're in here?" my husband asked as he shook my shoulders.

I opened my eyes and looked through him. "They're so hungry. But more than that, they're in pain. There's so many of them and they're hurting each other."

"Fuck," he grumbled.

"We need to get the hell out of here!" shouted Sam.

"No, it's too late. They're everywhere," I gasped as I stood, my legs shaky.

The intensity of the wind increased and the walls threatened to give way. A brief lull preceded a palpable change in air pressure that soon built into a shrill howl.

"The crawlspace! Back bedroom, now!" Sam shouted, fighting to be heard over the noise outside.

I didn't question him. My heart pounding, I held onto his outstretched hand and followed him through the kitchen and down the hallway. I reached my other hand back until Gus found it. The agitation of the storm stirred dust long hidden within the walls, annoyingly surrounding us as it fell to the floor. I coughed as we fought to get to the bedroom. Living in the Pacific Northwest, our only real threat had ever been the big earthquake everyone said was overdue. Even so, I knew what was trying to claim our lives. It wasn't the eruption of Mt. Rainier. It wasn't the Roamers that surrounded us. It wasn't the expected "big one" that was so overdue. At that moment my name may as well have been Dorothy, but I'd be damned if I was going to visit somewhere over the rainbow.

We rounded the corner and raced to the bedroom that was nearest the end of the hall. Sam had left his battery operated lantern behind while he was trying to sleep, and it now lay on its side on the floor. Sam broke his hold on my hand and rushed to pull back a tattered area rug that sat in the middle of the small room. The screaming outside grew louder, if that was possible. The outer walls of the house were being battered.

"Hurry! Get in!" yelled Sam as he pulled open a panel in the floor of the closet.

Long shadows from the tipped-over lantern made the opening in the floor appear warped. Going below the house was not something I wanted to do. I had no idea what was down there, how far down the bottom might be, or how secure it was from the dead. Sam lowered himself down the hole first.

"Zoe, quick," Gus said to me calmly. He knew me well. He knew that panic would not go over well.

I crouched by the opening and hastily lowered my legs down. Sam's arms received me and before I had a chance to catch my breath he pulled me away from the opening. The sound of the wind wailing changed to include glass breaking and wood splintering.

"Gus!" I screamed.

"He'll make it down," Sam yelled as he continued to drag me from the opening.

On cue, the crawlspace filled with light from the lantern that had moments before been on the floor above us. Gus' hair was littered with dust and debris and blood poured down his face from a wound at his hairline.

"We've got to get away from the hatch!" screamed Sam.

The sound of the old farmhouse being ripped apart followed us as we ducked under beams and belly-crawled away from the opening in the floor. I balled my hands into fists and pushed myself forward as far as I could. Sam stopped, preventing me from gaining more than another foot of ground. Gus continued forward, covering my body with his own the best that he could. The weight of his body pressed me against the cold damp soil. I reached up and wrapped my hands around the back of my neck, trying to protect myself from anything that might fall on us. Time seemed to stand still as the horrific sounds of the tornado continued.

It all stopped as quickly as it had begun. Where floorboards had been moments before, cold water now rushed in at us. In the distance the growling of the tornado gradually faded.

.

"Gus?" I called out. I still felt him against me, clinging to me.

"I'm here. We need to move." He sounded near panic.

"Sam? Sam, are you okay?" I called out.

"Not sure," he called back. He sounded farther away than I recalled him being.

Gus pushed himself off of me. The pressure of his hands on my legs was uncomfortable.

"What does 'not sure' mean exactly, brother?"

"It's my arm. I think it's pinned."

"Where's the lantern?" I asked.

"Hell if I know," grunted Gus.

"What the hell happened?" I asked, even though I knew the answer.

"It was a fucking goddamned tornado. A tornado, in fucking Washington State!" replied Gus.

"Sam, can you tell what's pinning you?" I asked.

I heard the man strain to free himself. "A beam, I'm guessing. This end of the room must have collapsed. Your end?"

"Gone," said Gus.

"We need to get out of here," I urged. Rain was falling heavily and cold water was pooling underneath me.

"I need to get past you, darlin'. I can't help Sam from here."

Gus, the crawlspace is starting to flood.

I didn't want Sam to overhear, so did my best to relay the information silently. Gus didn't answer.

"Did you hear me?" I asked aloud.

"No."

"There's a lot of water," I said, trying to keep the alarm out of my voice.

"Hang tight. I think I feel the lantern."

Light flickered and then suddenly surrounded us, indicating he had found it. Gus' appearance was alarming. The blood that ran down his face as he first entered the crawlspace was now coated with dirt and grime. His hair was disheveled and his eyes full of grave concern. Whatever was going on inside his head, I wasn't privy. The last time we had lacked connection I had been pregnant with Hope, and I was quite certain that was not the case now.

"It'd be awesome if you could hurry," said Sam, starting to sound panicked.

"It feels like we have company nearby," I said

"Zoe, talk to me," urged Gus as he struggled to crawl past me.

"They're scattered but starting to move toward us."

I moved backward, trying to give Gus more room. He was so much bigger than me and debris blocked his way.

"This is as far as I can go," Gus shouted. "Son of a fucking bitch! Sam, can you see what's pinning you?"

"Barely, but the light helps. Right now there's a shit load of mud pooling by my left shoulder. My right hand's caught under a collapsed beam. If I could roll that direction I think I could get it free. There's no goddamn fucking room to even rotate."

"I can't reach him," grumbled Gus through gritted teeth as he attempted to move aside collapsed flooring that blocked his way.

"You guys need to get out of here while you can," called out Sam. He was clearly in pain.

"Gus, let me squeeze through. Before it's too late," I said.

As he began to back up, I slithered by him. The flooding was worsening and I could feel the chill trying its best to slow me down.

"Hand me the light!" I urged. The situation was quickly turning beyond dangerous.

I reached back until I felt the plastic casing of the lantern. My fingers gripped the edge of the base; it had broken and painfully sliced my right index finger open. I winced, but didn't waste time in inspecting the wound.

"I'm almost there, Sam," I grunted as I forced myself farther under the collapsed floor.

Sam's feet were bare and coated in mud. He was twisted at the waist and struggling to free himself.

"If you can't get me out, head east," he grunted.

"We'll get you," I said sternly as I reached his side.

He ignored what I said. "There's an old root cellar built into the hillside. We have emergency packs in there. It's next to the ruins of an old smoke stack. Hard to miss."

"Lay on your back," I said. "I can't see your hand."

He flattened himself the best he could. His forehead was inches from a collapsed beam and the back of his head was surrounded with the sludge that was steadily rising. I wedged my torso across his and finally found his hand. It was pinned from the wrist to the ends of his fingers; only his pinky remained exposed. Blood pooled around his flesh.

"What a stupid fucking way to die," he grumbled.

"Shut up. You're not gonna die."

I wedged my own hands under the collapsed wood and concrete that pinned him down. Lacking space, I barely managed to get my fingertips under the edge.

"Seriously, though. A fucking stuck *hand*?"

"Sam, shut up. I can't get my hands under this crap. Can you wiggle your hand at all?"

I watched as his pinky flinched.

"Not really."

"Zoe, we need to hurry," urged Gus.

"I need to try to dig underneath his hand," I called back to him. "I need a knife or something."

"Don't cut it off," pleaded Sam.

I nearly choked. "I don't intend to. I just need to loosen the dirt underneath so you can slide it out. Gus?" I called out. "A knife would be awesome right now. Or even a freaking spoon!"

"Hold up, darlin'! Both of you keep quiet. We have company."

A chill ran up my spine. I still couldn't fully sense the creature that was approaching. I didn't know if it was one or more. I couldn't tell if it knew we were there. I struggled to turn from my already awkward position. The movement caused Sam to cry out harshly.

"Sorry," I whispered.

I looked back and watched as Gus pulled himself up through the opening in the ruined floor. The light from the lantern flickered as if the battery was struggling. The sound of rain continued to hammer down and the flow of sludge beneath us intensified. I knew that if I turned back to help Gus, Sam would drown.

"Go with him," Sam said through clenched teeth. I turned my head back to look at him and saw the pain on his face as his muscles tensed under the effort to free himself.

"I told you to shut up," I replied, irritated. "We're on our own for now, and so is Gus."

"My left back pocket. My pocket knife might still be there."

I inched over until my hand found his waist. It was impossible to see since his body was half submerged. Faintly, I could sense Gus' worry. He was afraid, but it was more than that. I frantically felt under the cold dirty water, searching for Sam's blade.

"It's not there, Sam!"

"You need to go," he spat. I looked at his face.

The waterline was close to his mouth I knew he was right, that I should go, but found myself unable to leave his side.

"Fuck it," I muttered as I stretched my body across his again.

Positioning was awkward. I needed both of my hands free, which meant putting all of my body weight on Sam. He was already having a hard time breathing.

"This is gonna hurt."

"It's useless. Just get your asses to the root cellar."

I ignored him and reached for his injured arm.

"Don't hurt me, Sam," I said through clenched teeth.

I wrapped both hands around the far end of his arm, where the flooring trapped him. He flinched beneath me, realizing what I was about to do. I dug my knees into the ground the best I could, but had such little room above me with which to work. I managed to lace my middle and index fingers together and pulled hard.

"Nooooooo!"

Sam's scream was earsplitting. It was followed by a half groaning, half crying. I felt his wrist cracking and crumbling beneath my hands. Knowing I wasn't strong enough to break bones in this situation, I could only assume it had broken during the floor's collapse.

"Stop!" he pleaded.

"It's the only way. You'll die if I stop," I shouted.

I pulled again, pausing only when his other hand met my side painfully. His fingers dug into my flesh, but the pain didn't stop me from pulling even harder.

"Zoe!" shouted Gus. "You have to get out of there!"

I took a deep breath, shoved a knee into Sam's side, and pulled one last time. The resulting scream shook me to my core. I hit my head on a beam when his hand at last came free.

"Sam, move!" I ordered. "I don't care how much your hand hurts, move now!"

My side ached horribly where his hand had squeezed me, and the bite wound on my butt was throbbing. My head hurt and sparkles of light littered my vision.

I backed up, only slowing to make sure Sam was following me. The crawlspace was even tighter for him and he was hindered by being one-handed and in agony. Mud made the way slippery and getting to the exit seemed to take an eternity. Eventually Gus' hands found me and with his help I emerged from the wet and cramped space.

The first rays of light were shining in the east and Gus was covered in blood.

"It's okay. It's a Roamer's, not mine," he assured me quickly.

I nodded. "Sam's gonna need help. His wrist is broken."

Our voices seemed to echo in the eerie stillness that was left behind by nature.

"I'm on it," he said.

I watched the horizon as Gus leaned down and grabbed Sam under his good arm. Gus strained as he pulled Sam topside.

"The root cellar," he huffed, out of breath.

"Gus, we have to head east. Sam said there's a root cellar built into the side of a hill with an emergency stash."

"Can you walk, brother?" Gus asked, looking intently at Sam. "You look like you've lost a lot of blood."

"Yeah. I'll be okay."

"Zo, we need to make a sling for his arm," Gus said.

The three of us looked at each other. None of us had been prepared to suddenly flee outside. We didn't have much time, so I slipped out of my muddy hoodie and used Gus' knife to slice the elastic section from the bottom of the sweatshirt.

"This'll have to do," I said as I reached up and hung the makeshift loop across his torso and helped lift his injured wrist into the other end. Sam looked pale and was breathing hard. I dropped the remainder of the wet shirt to the ground.

"Let's go," said Gus.

We set off in the direction of the rising sun. It was still too dark to make out much of the landscape, but we skirted around a fallen Roamer. Gus' handiwork, I was sure. By the time we reached the ruins of the smoke stack, Sam had slowed considerably and his pallor had worsened. Gus supported him as we continued east.

CHAPTER 10

The cellar wasn't much to speak of. Three of four walls were hard-packed earth. The rear was shorter than the front. The ceiling was little more than ill-fashioned two-by-fours and scrap metal. The front was made of a material which I had never seen before. Thankfully it was relatively dry inside. The door had been left unlocked, secured only by a bent nail and a loop made of twine. There was a dank smell to the heavily stagnant air. Transparent Rubbermaid totes were neatly stacked in the back left corner. They held bottles of what I assumed was water and several cans of food. Totes closer to the front were opaque but labeled "emergency packs."

"Up on the wall, grab a lantern," said Sam. He was clearly exhausted.

Gus was closest to the wall that had items hanging from nails and hooks. Wrenches, hammers, lanterns, screw drivers, some unusual homemade weapons that sported spikes, and rain jackets. As he picked the closest lantern, I lowered Sam to the dirt floor.

"Batteries are in with the emergency packs. Double bagged in Ziplocs."

"I'll grab them," I offered.

I squatted in front of the large totes and removed the lid from the one closest to the door. Inside were four backpacks, all plain black. They were heavy duty and looked like they were meant for hiking. A piece of thin plywood acted as an inner divider, separating the backpacks on the left and other supplies on the right. It was on the smaller right side that I found the bags of batteries.

"What size?" I asked.

"C's" answered my husband. "Four of them."

After a quick hand-off of batteries, Gus got the light going quickly. In the small space, it was rather effective. Unnerving long shadows were cast about, dancing as Gus walked toward the only door.

"We need to stay quiet," said Sam. "And we can't stay long. If they come, we'll be trapped in here."

"Ayup. I agree."

"I need pain pills. Can one of you grab the first aid kit?"

"Sure. Where is it?"

"The bin next to the batteries. With the white lid."

Since I was closest, I twisted until I could reach the bin. As I took the lid off, I jumped back, startled.

"Shit!" I yelped.

A dingy looking opossum scurried farther into the corner.

"Don't move," whispered Gus.

"Fuck that," I replied, scooting away from the bin and the overgrown marsupial.

"Hold still, darlin'. I'm serious."

I sat there, next to Sam, and watched the shadowy corner. Nothing happened. I didn't look behind me when I heard Gus rustling with the items on the far wall.

"Don't move too fast," mumbled Sam.

"I won't. If we're lucky it's playing 'possum," answered Gus in his hushed voice.

Gus proceeded toward where the creature was last seen. He had to hunch slightly to clear the low ceiling.

"Zoe, I need you to pull the supply bin back."

"Why?"

"So I can kill it."

"Don't let it run at me," I ordered.

"Ayup."

I changed position and stood on my knees. I reached forward and pulled on the plastic container. The opossum hissed loudly, but was silenced as soon as Gus brought a hammer down hard on its head. He gave it a second whack for good measure, then turned toward us with a big grin on his face.

"Dinner," he said with a wink.

He pulled his hunting knife from the sheath on his belt and quickly set to field dressing the dead animal. I turned away, not out of disgust, but to find the first aid kit. Sam's breathing was heavy and by the way his face was contorting I knew he was miserable. The bin was well organized. Thermal emergency blankets on the left, IV bags and supplies in the middle, vials of medication that I recognized as antibiotics, and three white plastic cases with red crosses on their fronts. I grabbed the one on top.

"There should be an ace wrap in each case and the pain pills are in the compartment in the lid," muttered the injured man.

I opened the case and grabbed a bottle of pills.

"Gus, tell me which ones are for pain," I said.

"Read 'em off."

"Doxycycline, Lorazepam, Diphenhydramine, Oxycodone. The Oxy, right?"

"Ayup. What milligrams are they?"

"Five."

"Give him two of those and one of the Lorazepam. It'll help him relax."

I popped the lid on the bottle of Oxycodone and picked up the bottle of Lorazepam. "These say half a milligram," I said for good measure.

"The Lorazepam?"

"Yeah."

"Shit. Give him four."

"You sure?"

"Ayup. That's a really low dose."

I fished out the rest of the pills. Both the lorazepam and oxycodone looked nearly identical: small, white, and round. I grabbed a bottle of water from the stash at the back of the cellar before approaching Sam with his pain relief. By the time I got back to him, he had slumped against one of the bins, his eyes closed. His left hand supported a very swollen and bruised right wrist.

"Sam," I said gently.

His eyes immediately shot open and he looked at me intensely.

"It's okay. It's just me. Gus said to take these for the pain."

"Thanks," he said, his voice cracking. "Water first? My throat's so dry."

"His wrist is swelling, Gus" I said as I handed Sam the bottle of water.

"Did you find ACE wraps?" asked Gus.

"Yeah."

"Can you wrap it? Mid fingers to mid forearm? Not too tight, but snug. It'll help keep the swelling down."

I didn't answer, but fished a wrap from the first aid kit.

"Sam…"

"I heard," he said. "Go ahead."

"Swallow these."

I handed him the six pills. He tossed them all into his mouth at once and took a large pull from the bottle. A very faint tickle began within my mind, originating from far off. It was unmistakable the dead.

"Stay quiet?" I looked at him to make sure he understood.

"I'll be done here in a minute, Zo. I can help with his wrist."

"Thanks."

The thought I picked up from Gus was vague, but I knew he was worried that Sam might involuntarily hurt me in the heat of his pain if I were to wrap his wrist.

"Let the pills kick in for a few minutes before we get started. Can you look around for dry clothes?"

"Sam? Are there any here?" I asked.

He nodded. "Back by the bins of water. There's some of those big plastic vacuum-seal storage bags like they used to advertise on TV. It's hard to see from here but there's a shelf hidden up under what looks like the back ceiling. You'll see how to open the hatch once you get up there. There's some dried meat too, and cans of nuts."

I lifted myself off the ground to a crouch, leaned forward and kissed him on the cheek. "I'm really sorry about your wrist."

He looked back at me and forced a smile. "You saved my life."

Without saying any more, I stood and found my way to the back of the cellar. Built into the back dirt wall was a plywood door that was well camouflaged. A small bit of twine hung from the side. Tugging, the board fell outward and to the ground. Luckily, I stepped back in time so it didn't land on my feet. The cavity behind the board was larger than I expected. It filled with light as Gus approached me from behind, lantern in hand.

"We need to get out of here soon," I said quietly.

"How soon?"

"Ten minutes max. I don't think they know we're here, but they're getting closer."

"We all need dry clothes. We should be okay without masks or bandanas, until this sludge dries. The rain was at least good for that."

"Whoever packed this was well organized. These are all labeled. You and Sam are about the same size, right? XL?"

"Yeah that sounds about right."

"Here." I handed him a clear plastic bag. "I'll find mine, just get down to Sam and dig through those. I'll bring food down with me."

"I'll start bandaging his wrist. Get dressed and throw a first aid kit into one of the emergency packs."

"Should I grab them all extras?"

"How many are there?"

"Three."

"Just take one. We need to leave something in case anyone else needs it later."

As he walked away, I grabbed a collapsed bag that was labeled "women's medium." I also tucked a bag of what I assumed was fish jerky under the crook of my arm, and filled my other hand with a can of mixed nuts.

It took us just under ten minutes to find clothing, dress, wrap Sam's wrist, and pack. By then the dead were too near for my comfort. The only shoes I found were a size too large for Sam, but better than being barefoot. I helped put them on his feet while Gus bandaged his hand and fashioned a sling. He was clearly still in pain but said the pills were beginning to help. The dead opossum hung from Gus' belt, tied shut in a plastic bag. We slipped out the front of the cellar, into daylight. The massive devastation from the tornado was visible to us at last. The old farmhouse in the distance was flattened except for one corner, which leaned treacherously to one side. Circular patterns were etched into the now-wet ash. Long shadows pointed westward as the sun was still trying to take its place in the sky.

"Which way?" Gus asked.

"North-east. There's a small church not too far out of our way. We need to get out of this muck."

"I'm down for that," replied Gus.

"There they are," I interrupted. "Look on that ridge."

In the distance, to the south, was a huge line of crowd of the dead clumsily making their way toward us. Their path was downhill and several fell on their way down, sliding and rolling sloppily.

"It's the sludge," said Gus. "It's slowing them down."

***

We moved forward, taking care to not slip. We had speed on our side, but the slurry still made the going difficult. The only blessing was a lack of dust in the air, allowing us to breathe without filtering the air. As the sun grew high in the sky, the warmth slowed us down.

"How much farther?" I asked, my throat dry.

"Just about another mile," said Sam, a bit out of breath. "Let's keep going. We can rest when we get there."

"Right," I said simply, not wanting to talk.

***

That last mile somehow turned into ten. Thanks to the sun, the sludge that resulted from the storm dried; caked and forming cracks, it resulted in a soft crunching sound as we walked. The smell of sun mixed with that of burnt earth and putrefaction. The church never intersected with our path. Sam finally announced we were off course when we happened upon the outskirts of Wenatchee. While the landscape was alien as a result of Mother Nature's wrath, he recognized a McDonald's and gas-station combination. The surrounding buildings were in ruins, half of them burnt and the rest claimed by the elements after being left exposed by looters.

"This is farther than our group's ventured on supply runs. We don't have a safe house this end of town. I can't guarantee this building's clear of the dead."

"What'd you estimate the distance is from here to your people?" asked Gus.

"We've gone farther east than I meant to. So another half day at most."

"Let's get inside. There's Roamers nearby," I said.

I wrapped my arms around myself and shivered, despite the heat from the sun.

"I think our best bet is the gas station. It's a lot smaller than the McDonald's," offered Sam.

"Ayup. I agree. Plus, the McDonald's has a pane of glass busted out."

I stepped forward first, wanting to get out of view of any dead eyes that might be watching. The front door of the gas station was crackled as if someone had tried to break in but failed. I pushed on the horizontal bar to find the door locked tight. Alerted by the sudden sounds of my attempted entry, a large rodent scurried across the floor inside. Bits of wrappers and food littered the floor, as well as rodent feces and areas of brown liquid. As I peered through the glass door, I realized there was movement everywhere. The place was infested with rats. They had claimed the small convenience store for their own and were feasting on old snack food like Templeton at a carnival.

"It's a no-go," I said ominously.

"What's up?" asked Gus as he and Sam got closer. I noticed he was supporting Sam, who looked like he was ready to pass out.

"Rats. Everywhere."

"I don't think we have much choice," said Sam.

"There's too much rat crap in there. It's a cesspool of filth," I said, looking at Gus.

"Sam, is there anything else close by?"

"Around the corner. A library." He sounded out of breath.

"Let's head out," said Gus.

***

The library was still standing, despite most of the rest of the block having been burnt. Set back from the main street, it was a small building at just one level. Like everything else, the lawn had gone wild and shrubs had dried from lack of human attention. We cautiously approached the front door of the structure and found it locked.

"Sam, we need to leave you here while we look for a way in," I said. "We won't be long."

Gus and I helped him slide to the ground and he leaned against the entryway. He nodded his head briefly. I looked at Gus, and knew by his strained face that he was worried about Sam.

We left our packs with our new friend and proceeded around the closest corner. The windows along the side of the building were tall and narrow and not designed to open. There were two single metal doors on the backside of the building but both were locked and opened outward with concealed hinges.

Gus leaned down and picked up a river rock that appeared to have been left out as a door prop. "Stand back," he instructed me.

"What are you doing?"

"Breaking in."

I stepped aside and he hurled the rock at one of the narrow windows. The shattering glass was astonishingly loud. I held my breath, waiting for the dead to pour out of the opening. Stale air escaped the long-closed-up building. The air was rank of mildew and damp paper and made me cough.

"I need to get back to Sam. Leaving him alone like he is feels wrong."

"Be careful. I'll go in and unlock the front door for you. If I need to find a key, it may take a while. If there's any trouble and I haven't shown up, head back here and come in through the window, even if it means leaving him."

"I can't just leave Sam," I said.

"Yes, you can. If it means your staying alive."

"Just…hurry."

He leaned down and kissed me softly on the lips. Heat radiated from his skin and his familiar smell made my heart skip a beat. I wrapped my arms around him and returned the kiss. I broke the embrace and turned to re-join Sam. Stopping to look back at Gus, I said simply "be safe."

He nodded once and disappeared through the broken window.

By the time I reached Sam, he was slumped to the side and sleeping. I was beginning to wonder if there was more wrong with him than a broken wrist. I crouched down next to the man and unzipped the backpack. I rummaged through and quickly found a full bottle of water. I drank half quickly before returning the lid and tucking it back in with other supplies. While I was sure it had been less than a minute since I left Gus, it felt like forever. I watched in the distance for any signs of danger. My senses were off, making me unsure if the occasional ache in my hip or ripple of electricity deep within my mind were the dead nearby or not. Shadows began to play tricks with my eyes. A breeze picked up and the vegetation surrounding us began to dance erratically. An old oak tree, still bare of leaves for the season, loomed in the distance. Its branches reached out like skeletal fingers and two large knots halfway up the trunk looked like old eyes that had seen many secrets over the years. I kept my gaze focused on those wooden snarls, allowing my peripheral vision to watch for any subtle movements. I was sure something ran by on the left. Maybe a coyote or a feral dog or cat. A bird chattering in a nearby shrub suddenly fell silent. The only sound was the whisper of the wind, which faded suddenly. The stillness that fell around us was alarming. I finally moved my eyes toward the last movement I had seen, finding nothing unusual.

"Sam," I whispered, hoping to wake him.

I didn't want to take my eyes off the backdrop, so reached blindly toward him until I found his shoulder.

"Sam, wake up."

I felt his arm tense.

"Where are we?" he asked.

"The library. Gus is inside – he should be over to unlock the door any minute. Stay awake, and stay quiet. Something feels off."

"Talk to me," he said.

"It's too quiet. The birds stopped chirping and I swear I saw something run to the north."

The sinking feeling in my belly grew and I wished that Gus would hurry.

"Maybe we should get to the end of the building. Gus broke a window. We can get in there," I said, my voice even quieter than before.

"I can feel them," Sam whispered.

"What do you mean?" I asked.

"It's in my back. Like electricity going up and down my spine."

He wasn't making sense. As far as we knew, he wasn't infected. Or hadn't been.

"Let's go."

"Don't gotta convince me," he replied.

I stood up, pulling Sam with me. The stillness and silence that surrounded us broke suddenly. A very small figure darted amongst the ruins of a park, ducking behind shrubbery. A giggle echoed, making the hair on the nape of my neck stand on end. I tugged on Sam's arm, encouraging him to follow me. We left our pack in a heap in the ground to save time. As soon as we left the limited shelter of the entryway, another figure flitted in the distance. I already knew what they were.

"Sam, listen carefully. Don't look them in the eyes."

"Why?" he asked as we began to move the length of the building, our backs against the brick face.

"They're monsters. They'll take away your will to move if you look them in the eyes."

"I'll take your word for it."

Not daring to take my eyes away from the overgrown park, I winced when my still-healing shoulder collided with a downspout. More giggling rang out as one of the dead began singing *Itsy Bitsy Spider Ran up the Waterspout*. How fitting. The singing was soon joined by a little boy's voice calling out…

"Molly…come out and play! Molly, Molly, Moll-ly, dead and burnt Moll-ly!" it chanted, mocking me.

"Shut up," I grumbled under my breath.

"What?" asked Sam.

I shook my head side to side. "I'll explain later. Just…"

My voice broke off when the sound of a little girl screaming cut through the heavy air that surrounded us. Sam fidgeted.

"From the right," he whispered. "You head to the window; I'll see if I can help her."

I grabbed onto his good arm. "No. It's not human."

"It sounds human. If there's any chance…" he said, pleading with me to listen.

"Molly -Molly- Moll-ly! Molly Molly, dead and gone! Moll-ly buried under some holly!"

This time it was a girl's voice.

"There's no chance. We have to get inside," I urged.

He looked at me for a painfully long moment before deciding to humor me. With a single nod, we turned the corner and continued to work our way to the window that would lead to Gus and, hopefully, safety. The occasional giggle rang out as shadows in the distance came to life. They seemed to be playing some twisted game of hide and seek.

"Sam, stop." I held a hand out as warning. "They're not going to let us get to the window. Gus should have opened the front door or come out by now."

"What should we do?" he whispered back to me.

"I'm not sure. These children – monsters – are playing some fucked up game. I'm not sure why they're hiding. I've never seen them do that before; usually they come out and do their mind-fuck thing."

"We should keep going," he suggested.

"They don't want us to," I said under my breath. "That's what it is. They don't want us to go inside."

I looked at my companion, who was closely watching the area across the street.

"Sam, inside, now! Run!"

We turned and ran toward the broken window. It was only twenty feet away, give or take. Our footfalls were loud on the pavement. More shadows came to life, finally revealing the monsters that hid around us. There were so many of them; more than I had seen gathered at once. The tallest of the dead children stood in front, as if guarding the smaller ones. It was clear now why they had been hesitant to show themselves. Their perfect little faces were no longer intact. Their youthful disguises had finally succumbed to the effects of decay. Ponytails and braids were disheveled and one of the boys in the front of the group was missing the skin from the entire left side of his face. At least seven sets of dead eyes stared at us from across the street. I knew there were many more eyes upon us, still out of our sight.

My head began throbbing as we approached a locked door that stood between us and the broken window. I looked back toward the crowd of rotting children. They were following us, but at a slow pace.

"They're herding us," said Sam.

"I know."

I needed time to think. Time we didn't have.

I could feel Gus in my core. He was near and I knew he was there at the window waiting. Along with the warmth of his soul, I felt urgency in his mind. Clearly, he knew something we didn't.

"Sam, faster!" I yelled.

The children stopped in their tracks, but for such a brief moment had I blinked I may have missed it. I picked up speed as they rushed forward. I knew they would be fast, but a quick look back showed them moving at alarming speed. I didn't have time to look for Sam, so trusted that he was right behind me. I didn't slow down till I got to the window, knowing even a split second could mean the difference between life and death. As I neared the window ledge, I gripped the edge with both hands. Pain seared my hands where broken glass gouged them. Gus was there to grab me. As he hastily pulled me through the opening, we fell to the floor. I rolled to the side, focusing my eyes back on the open window. The boy with only part of his face was already more than halfway through. His right forearm caught on a shard of glass. As the fragment bit into his rotting flesh, a foul odor rushed inward. I jumped to my feet and rushed forward in an attempt to push the creature back outside.

Empty eyes stared back at me. The creature opened its mouth and snarled. Its lips, or what was left of them, twisted awkwardly. A third of his mouth was gone, clearly showing a yellow and dried skull and broken teeth still clinging to jawbone. The opposite side sported dry and cracked skin that looked painful. He smelled unusual, of rot and sickly sweet flowers. The ugly snarl turned into an even uglier attempt at a smile. The other children hummed in the background as if taunting us. I didn't see Sam anywhere. Before I could do much harm to the dead boy, Gus leapt in front of me and shoved the creature hard.

"Help me move the book case!" he yelled as the dead juvenile fell backwards into the emaciated and decaying arms of his companions.

I looked at Gus briefly. His left cheek was bleeding from a wound that ran from the middle of his cheek to near the corner of his mouth, just above his beard-line. He was straining against a nearby bookshelf, attempting to slide it in front of the broken window. I rushed forward to assist him, nearly tripping over my own feet as I passed the commotion at the window. The boy with half a face was already back on his feet, now joined by a girl who wore a mask of rot and maggots. Her left eye had been eaten away, leaving only a putrid socket crusted in black and brown and green. My heart was pounding as I stood next to Gus and helped push the shelf. It was heavy and my sore shoulder protested loudly.

"As soon as we have the sons of mother fuckers blocked out, head to the door behind the main desk," grunted Gus.

"Sam…"

"We can't do anything for him," said Gus quickly.

I knew he was right.

The shelf finally budged and began to slide. It almost fell forward, but Gus reacted quickly enough to tip it back up. It made a resounding *thud* when it crashed back against the dead who were still making an effort to climb inside. I felt the anger of the dead. They had an innocence to their minds. They were angry that we were slipping from their grip. They had walked away from the one who was in charge of them. Shreds of their memories crept into my head. They had been taken care of all this time, by an old woman who was neither Roamer nor Runner nor Alive. She was something we had yet to encounter. That fact worried me the most. They had feared her, and had strived to be perfect for her. In the end, their hunger for fresh flesh had won out. They waited until their numbers grew large enough, and then overtook her. In the end, the creature was dismembered by the dead children. The images that flashed through my mind were disturbing and my stomach reeled.

"Zo, the shelf's not gonna hold. Get to the door behind the desk!"

I knew from his tone and his rudimentary emotions that he meant for me to get to safety while he stayed behind.

"Not without you!" I yelled.

"One of us has to make it back to Hope," he said as he strained to hold the shelf up with his back.

"Then let's secure the shelf and both make it out," I said, my voice filling with fear and anger.

"We have nothing to tie it down, darlin'. No way to secure it."

He looked at me with wide eyes. His body jolted from the dead fighting against him.

The cracking of gunfire outside made me jump. There were at least two different guns firing, if not three. Gus and I looked at each other without speaking. The shreds of memories inside my mind, the ones not belonging to me, slowed down. My soul could feel each of their lives as the undead twinkled out one by one. By the time it was over, which couldn't have been more than a couple of minutes, I was exhausted. The gunfire ended abruptly. I fell to my knees and looked up at Gus. He was still standing with his back to the shelf but his posture was more relaxed. He held a finger up to his lips, encouraging me to stay quiet. Having no issues with that, I nodded.

I took a few deep breaths and listened. The quiet was maddening. I forced myself up off the floor. Gus wore a look of concern, his gaze fixed to my side. I looked down only to see dark crimson dripping from my fingertips. As I looked back up at Gus, the room spun and colors faded.

CHAPTER 11

Sleep. I was asleep and it felt so good. I could hear the clinking of someone stirring something; metal on glass? I wanted to open my eyes, but the desire to sleep won. Someone was nearby. I could hear muffled voices in the distance. A man and a woman whose voice was so familiar.

"Emilie?" I called out.

I forced my eyes open and tried to sit up. Searing pain in my arm made me cry out. A large white bandage covered my forearm. Nothing made sense. My mouth and eyes were dry, my hand hurt like hell, and I had just called out for my best friend. No. Emilie was dead. She had been gone for a long time now. Gus. I was with Gus.

"Gus?" I called out, keeping my voice low.

I blinked until my vision cleared. I was on a stretcher with an IV in my arm. I was in a room made of concrete and tile. It reminded me of the P.E. shower room back in high school. My head swam, forcing me to lay back down.

"I'm here, darlin."

Gus walked through a door-less entry, his face looking grim.

"Lay down, love. You've lost a lot of blood and I don't want you fainting. You've been out for a couple days."

"What happened?" I asked, my voice catching from a dry throat.

"Bad luck," he said as he sat on a rolling stool next to the stretcher. "Sam's friends showed up and killed off the herd that was trying to get into the library. A stray bullet hit your forearm."

"Now tell me the bad news," I said, half-joking.

He put his elbows on his knees and clasped his hands. His face was slack, except for his forehead. He wore the telltale sign of stress and worry; wrinkling of his brow. It was an odd expression of which I doubt he was aware. I'd seen it before, far too many times.

"Gus? What is it?"

After a long pause, he looked up at me. His eyes were red-streaked and his eyelids swollen.

"You've been crying," I said.

He hung his head again and sighed deeply.

"There's just been a lot of shit happening," he said, trying to dismiss his emotions.

"Where are we?"

"An old concrete warehouse a bit south of Wenatchee. It looks like maybe it used to be part of a farm. Turns out Sam's group set it up as an infirmary a couple weeks ago when several of them got sick."

"Sick with what?"

"Sounds like it was a nasty stomach bug. They lost one of the babies and the two eldest in the group; a husband and wife who were both going on their eighty-second birthdays."

"Why are we here? Why not at their camp?"

"This is it. It's all that's left. Fourteen people, one dog, and a handful of supplies."

I sat up as far as I could without getting too dizzy. "Hope. Where is she?"

"She's okay. She's here, just a few rooms down. She's tired and anxious to see you."

"Bring her to me?"

"Of course. I just wanted to fill you in first. Their camp was overrun by Roamers. There were thirty-nine of their people there when it happened, Zoe. Thirty-nine, including Hoot and Hope."

"Oh God, Hoot? Is he…?" my voice trailed off.

"Alive. He was with the few who made it out."

"Thank God," I said quietly.

"Okay. Before I bring Hope in, you need to know her left arm is wrapped in gauze. Don't you panic, she's okay."

"What happened?"

"When they were escaping from the horde, she cut her arm on a chain link fence. Hoot said she was very brave during it all."

"Bring her to me, please."

He nodded but made no effort to stand.

"You look tired, Gus."

"Yeah, it's been a rough couple of days. Add donating blood and I'm pretty wiped."

I looked at my arm and followed the IV line to where a bag hung on the wall behind me. "That's yours?" I asked, indicating the blood.

"Ayup. Well, it's yours now. You lost a lot before we got you here."

"Did you ever find Sam?"

He nodded. "Yeah. I still don't know how he did it one-handed, but he managed to climb an old oak tree. Other than a broken wrist and scraped up knee he seems okay. Pretty shaken, but we all are."

Tired, I laid back down on the stretcher. He leaned forward, resting his head just below my chest. I put my hand on his head and stroked his hair. I hadn't realized I was cold until the heat from his closeness caused me to shiver.

"I'm so tired of it all," he mumbled against me. "So tired of it all."

He kept his head against me and began crying.

"Shhhh," I tried to soothe him. "Gus, what's wrong?"

"So many people died today. It just never ends. It's all just…death."

"No…"

"Yes," he sniveled.

"There's always life. It used to be just you and me…remember?"

He didn't answer.

"Look at me," I said.

He tilted his head so that he could see me. He had dark circles under his tear-filled eyes. I ran my palm across his cheek. His beard had grown so long that it hid how gaunt his cheeks had become.

I continued. "We've made life, Gus. We have Hope. Her name stands for so much and we have to always believe it's all worth it. It's not just death out there."

He closed his eyes and drew a deep breath.

"It's all too much," he said as he closed his eyes.

Before I had a chance to ask him to elaborate, the moment was interrupted by throat-clearing at the doorway. I looked up to see the most beautiful sight: Hoot holding our little Hope. Smiling, I reached my free arm out for her.

"Hi, baby," I said in a soothing voice.

Our daughter turned away, burying her head against Hoot's chest.

"Hope, honey, come see mama," said Gus.

Hoot rubbed her back while he carried her closer. She whimpered a couple of times before Gus took her from our friend.

"It's okay, Little Bug. It's just mama."

She peeked around Gus at me. A frown developed as she pointed at my arm.

"It hurts," she said with tears beginning to fill her eyes.

I forced a smile. "It's okay baby," I whispered. "Mama's okay."

"No, mama. It hurts."

Gus looked intently into her eyes. "Mama's alright."

"Mama's arm hurts," she said.

"Zoe? Do you need pain meds?" Gus asked.

"If you have any. But it's not that bad. I can go without."

"Hoot? Mind taking Hope for a few minutes?"

"Nah man, it's no problem." He reached for Hope, who seemed relieved to climb back into his arms.

"Can we go see Aum?" she whispered.

"Sure thing, Jellybean." Hoot looked at me. "I'll bring her back in half an hour or so?"

I nodded. As badly as I wanted to hold her, I let her decide what she was comfortable with.

"See ya later baby," I said weakly.

Hoot left with her and I sunk down into the bed. My arm was screaming at me, but I hadn't wanted to admit that in front of Hope.

"It's bad?" asked Gus.

I nodded. "Yeah."

"Hang tight. I'll grab some morphine for both you and Sam. He's about due."

"Thanks."

"Don't thank me yet. As soon as your transfusion is done, we need to leave here. It's just not safe."

I groaned. "Hey. Who's Aum?"

"It's what Hope calls Autumn."

I closed my eyes and listened as his footfalls led him from the small, dank room. The sound of thunder clapped outside. Wind blew in through an old broken-out window, carrying with it the scent of rain to come. The passage of time seemed to stand still. My arm throbbed with each beat of my heart. I pictured Gus' face, trying to focus on something other than the pain of my injury.

***

I woke feeling heavy. My injured arm ached, but the intense pain had eased. Hope's sweet childhood scent, partly that of a fresh baby and partly sweaty toddler, surrounded me. I could feel her warm breath against my armpit. The room was dark, but I didn't need light to know my sweet girl was near. She was sleeping on my uninjured arm, which was tingling and numb. I haphazardly adjusted onto my side, bringing my bandaged arm with me. Hope whimpered quietly at being disturbed.

"It's okay, baby," I quietly soothed, sensing her concern. "I'm okay. Where's Daddy?"

"Daddy's with the sick man," she said as if it were the most normal sentence in the world. I wasn't used to her speaking in full sentences.

"Sam?"

She shook her head side to side. "Ray. Papa make Ray better."

A crash in the distance made us both jump. I hugged Hope close as we waited in the dark. I felt her breath quicken as the sound of footfalls filled the hallway. The curtain hanging in the doorway of the room whipped open wide, making us both jump. Light flooded the room, blinding us. Hope squirmed and whined, a telltale sign that the light hurt her pale eyes.

"You have to get up, quick!" boomed Hoot's voice.

"What's going on?" I asked as I struggled to sit up.

"You can't feel it?" he asked, surprised.

Hope began crying as he rushed toward us. She readily climbed into his arms. As soon as she was off of me, I took Hoot's arm and swung my legs over the edge of the stretcher. My head swam for a moment as I adjusted to sitting upright.

"One of them just turned," he explained. "He bit someone else. Bit onto their arm before they knew what the hell was going on."

"Who?" I asked, suddenly terrified that Gus may be the victim.

"I'm not sure. Gus just yelled for me to get you two out of here."

Two gunshots rang out, causing Hope to jump in Hoot's arms. Her thumb instantly went to her mouth. I looked down at my arm. The IV was gone and the bandage was clean and. Gus must have changed it.

I tossed my blanket aside and stood.

"Turn right and head down the hallway," Hoot said. "There's a door at the far end. There's a school bus waiting outside just to the left. As soon as you're on board I'll hand Hope over to you."

Before he finished speaking, we were well on our way down the dark hallway. The only light came from battery-operated stick-it lights that clung to the walls about every fifteen feet. Someone in the distance screamed. It sounded like a woman, but the agony within the sound made it impossible to tell for sure. As I reached the door at the end of the hall, I paused. Hoot bumped into me as I came to a stop. The screaming continued.

"I have to get Gus," I choked out as Hoot looked at me as if I were certifiably insane.

"No. He and the others will meet us at the bus. If they're not here there in three minutes, I'll go back."

He pressed the metal bar on the door and followed us out into the night.

"Mama we go home now?"

I looked at her quickly and shook my head side to side.

"Baby, stay quiet until we're on the bus, okay?"

She nodded once and then shoved her thumb back into her mouth. The bus was several yards away. Not far beyond was a group of four Roamers staggering in our direction. Wind blew steadily, carrying with it the stench of rot and mud.

"Get on board," Hoot barked as we rushed to the folding door of the vehicle.

By the look of it, it had been a school bus at some point. Yellow paint showed through black paint that had been applied haphazardly. Iron bars ran vertically over the windows. The door had been replaced with a large piece of sheet metal, painted dark green. It was obvious someone had attempted to camouflage the rig. Hoot used his free arm to disengage a slide-lock at the top edge of the door, allowing him to pull it open.

"Climb in, quick!" he hollered.

I didn't need to be told a second time. Instinct drove me up the steps. As soon as I was halfway up, I turned and reached for Hope. The growls and moans of the dead were alarmingly close. Instead of handing her to me, Hoot clung to her as he himself climbed the stairs.

"Pull the chain on the door!" he shouted.

Hope began crying loudly. I looked around for a chain, finding it overhead. The first Runner was already to the door opening and lurched in toward us. The bottom step caught it in the shins, forcing it forward onto its face.

"Hoot!" I yelled. "I can't get it the door!"

A gunshot rang out to my left, from in front of the bus. I looked quickly and saw a man with whom I was unfamiliar. He was clean-shaven and wore jeans and a gray Henley top. He held a pistol, aimed in our general direction. Four more shots fell the remaining three creatures. As he ran toward the bus, others were running from the building.

"Clear the bodies!" I heard Gray Henley shout.

"Zoe, let them get it. Head to the back of the bus."

I looked down the long bus aisle to the back, where Hoot was doing his best to comfort my daughter. Only the first four rows of bench seats remained. They rest had been replaced with boxes of what I assumed were emergency supplies. On my right were two couches bolted to the floor. A smaller loveseat spanned the width of the back, right in front of the rear emergency exit. Hoot sat with Hope as the others kicked aside bodies and began rushing on board. I sat beside him and took Hope. I desperately searched the line of boarding strangers for Gus. A woman in her later years collapsed onto one of the longer sofas, coughing and trying to catch her breath. The smell of vomit and smoke accompanied the small crowd, making my nose and eyes burn. Hope continued to keen softly. I held her close and kissed the top of her head.

"Mama…baby Canda," Hope whimpered.

"She'll be here soon," Hoot assured her.

"No. Baby Canda not cry," she whined. "She cry and they go to sleep."

The infant that Sam had mentioned earlier.

I was so relieved when I finally saw Gus stagger aboard. His face was coated in black soot and he, too, was coughing. The noise from people yelling, crying, coughing, and tripping over each other's feet grew louder.

"I bet Autumn has baby Canada," Hoot said to Hope.

"Aum," she said with a quivering little chin. "Want Aum."

Gus rushed toward us, awkwardly walking around the others that were in his way. His front was covered in blood and soot. I stood and walked toward him. Once he did, he wrapped his arms around me.

"We need to leave," he whispered to me.

"Who's driving? And where's Sam?" I asked.

"Sam's heading out. Autumn has his back."

"Baby Canda," Hope whimpered as she looked wide-eyed at her dad.

"She'll be on the next bus, Sweet Girl," Gus said.

I knew that baby Canada was dead, if not from Gus' raw emotion then from the strained look on his angular face. Hope cried quietly, as if she were trying to hide her distress. I knew instinctively that she too had picked up on Gus' deep sadness. I held her tight and sat back on the couch. Gus joined us.

Two men stood outside at the back of the bus, on point with rifles. I looked to Gus for an indication of what was to come next. He didn't meet my gaze. Gunfire rang out behind us. Stealing a quick look out the emergency exit behind our loveseat, the two men on lookout were quickly making their way to the front of the bus. A girl in her teens cried out. "They're coming!"

The gunmen boarded and quickly pulled the door panel shut, securing it by wrapping a chain to the stair handrail.

"Papa!" Hope wailed. "Flower! Sam! I want Aum!"

On cue, Sam and Autumn came stumbling from the building. She carried a small blonde dog under one arm and was helping support Sam with her other. A Roamer stood between them and the entry to the bus. It was overly ripe with rotten flesh hanging from bone. They yelled for help, their cries mixing with a deep growl from the dead man that was now focused on them. The little dog barked wildly.

"Open the door!" I yelled out. "Help them!"

The armed men turned and looked at me.

"Fuck," one of them mumbled. He bent down to look out the windshield. I followed his gaze and saw several figures approaching.

"Gus, they can't open the door," I whispered. "They look like Runners."

Gus stood. "Hope, go to Uncle Hoot."

She was still trying to breathe between sobs, but allowed Hoot to take her from me.

"Don't open it," I cried out. "They're too fast."

"Any other way on board?" Gus shouted out.

"There's a ladder on the back. If they can get that we can bring them in through the top hatch," replied the woman who reeked of vomit.

"Keep the Roamer focused on Autumn and Sam," Gus hollered.

He walked to a window and carefully lowered it on its tracks. The bars on the outside would not allow for the trio to climb in, but I knew that Gus only meant to kill the Roamer, who was rapidly advancing toward Autumn, Sam, and the dog. My husband took aim through the bars, focusing the end of his pistol on the Roamer.

"I need them to get closer before I shoot it," he mumbled. "Zo, I'm going to get its attention. When I do, yell for Sam and Autumn to run to the back ladder. Tad, get ready to start the engine and everyone else hold on," he called forward.

I stood and quickly made my way to the window closest to the back. The stacked boxes made reaching the locking device on the window difficult, but I managed. The pane lowered with a squeal. I scrambled to the top of the box pile, knocking a few over. Once to the top, I pressed my face to the opening at the top of the window.

"Wait till I get it to face me, then call out the instructions," Gus said without looking my way. His eyes remained focused on the end of his firearm. "I'll be focused on any of the Runners who try to rush us."

I took a deep breath, ignoring the cries from my own daughter, and prepared to help. The plan seemed riddled with holes and I felt trapped inside the bus, unable to help. I also didn't want to leave these people behind.

"Hey you dead fuckers!" Gus yelled out through his window. "Come get us!"

The creature turned toward the sound of his voice, but did not leave its position.

"Come on you fucker!" he yelled again.

"It's not going to work. The Runners are keeping it on target," I said mournfully. Even without being able to sense them, I knew how the Runners worked.

"Sam, Autumn, I'm going to shoot this son of a bitch. You need to move toward the back of the bus and climb the ladder as soon as I fire. Understand?"

I saw Sam nod in understanding.

"You won't have much time before the faster ones are on you. Just get up the ladder and to the hatch up top. On my mark…"

Three heartbeats later his gun kicked and the resulting sound of the chamber unloading rang out, adding to the tension. The Roamer fell and was still while the man and woman rushed to the back of the bus. Through the rearmost window we watched as Autumn began her ascent one-handed, as her other clutched the small dog. Sam was right behind her, also one-handed from his broken wrist. I glanced forward and saw that the Runners were already to the middle of the bus. I watched in horror as three of them began scaling the sides of the bus, not bothering to follow their prey up the ladder. They were agile beyond what we'd seen before, making the climb aboard look like child's play.

"Oh my God," the woman wearing vomit cried out. "Oh my God they're gonna get in!" She was near hysteria.

Gus left his place at the window and rushed to the top hatch. My stomach sank, knowing he was about to play hero. As I watched, he climbed onto the back of a bench seat and unlatched the hatch before hefting himself up and partway through.

I didn't have time to cry out in protest. Three more shots rang out, each time resulting in a loud "thud" against the thin metal roof. Gus stepped down as Autumn's legs lowered into the cabin. He grabbed her around the waist as he lowered her to the floor, the dog still under her arm. The animal struggled to climb out of her grasp once it spotted Hope. The bus shuddered as the engine roared to life. Sam clambered down from the hatch, landing hard on his side. Gus maneuvered around him to secure the hatch, which like the front door was held in place by a chain.

"Everyone hold on!" shouted Gray Henley. "It's gonna get bumpy!"

Sam struggled to sit upright, wincing as he jarred his splinted wrist against the seat behind him. Those left standing all either sat or held onto something secure. The first several yards of our drive to the unknown were met with many bumps and collisions with the dead. Roamers continued to attempt to climb on board, but their efforts were met with iron bars and locked entries. Soon after departing, the speed of the bus left them behind.

CHAPTER 12

The ride away from the old concrete building was somber. Few people spoke for the first several miles. Hope remained on Hoot's lap, with Autumn and Flower at her side. My darling had calmed once Autumn was safely aboard, but her pale little face still wore a look of deep sadness.

"Hope? Do you want to sit with me?" I asked.

She shook her pudgy little face side-to-side and clung to Autumn. In that moment, a sadness fell upon my heart. Looking around, I saw weary faces and broken people. Gus stood near the front of the bus, talking with the driver. Once we left behind the dampness from the prior rain, ash began to billow behind us, leaving an unsettling trail. The dead walked aimlessly in the distance, albeit much slower than we'd grown to expect. I knew they were all Roamers by the way they walked haphazardly. At one point we passed a Roamer crouched down on the side of the road eagerly eating what looked like a skinned chupacabra. Gray Henley slowed the bus to circumvent an old abandoned vehicle that was covered in a thin layer of ash.

I turned my attention to Hope when she made a noise of disgust.

"Baby, what's wrong?"

She plugged her nose and looked at me. "Flower pooted."

As she spoke the words, the burn of dog flatulence bit my nose.

"He probably needs to go to the bathroom," I said. "I'll let your Papa know."

I smiled at her and walked to the front of the bus, where Gus was busy talking to the driver.

"Gus, I think the dog needs to go to the bathroom."

"It's probably as good a time as any to stop for a break," said the driver.

Gus turned to face everyone and cleared his throat.

"We haven't seen the dead in a while. Now's a good time to take a break. If you need help getting on or off the bus, raise your hand. If your hand isn't raised, try to help someone who needs it." He sounded so tired. "Stay within fifty feet or so."

"Hope, let's go," I said quietly.

She shook her head. She looked fearful. "No Mama. No touch."

I was perplexed. "Hope, I'm not going to hurt you."

"No Mama. No."

My heart broke as I looked at my daughter, not understanding what she was afraid of. She clung tightly to Autumn, trying to put distance between herself and me. Hoot stood and set his hand on my shoulder.

"Let Autumn take her?" he said, not quite asking and not quite instructing.

I looked at him, doing my best to keep my face neutral.

"I'll stay with them. She'll be safe," he said, trying to reassure me.

I reached to touch the top of Hope's head, a gentle gesture I had done since she was just new. She flinched and shrunk farther away.

"Hope, it's okay," Autumn said lovingly.

"No, Aum. No hurt Mama."

Gus joined us at the rear of the bus. As others began to leave the safety of the vehicle, he wrapped an arm around my waist. Hope sniffled and tightened herself against Autumn.

"We need to hurry," said Gus.

"Hope's a bit attached to Autumn right now," I explained.

"I'm headed out with them," continued Hoot.

"Thanks, brother. Let's get to it, come on, all of you, Hope, Autumn, Zoe. We all need a bathroom break."

***

As the miles passed, the layer of ash on the ground had grown sparse. The sun was straight overhead, finally warming the day to a tolerable temperature. The air smelled clean, as if death had yet to touch the area. I watched as Hoot and Autumn carried Hope to the shoulder of the roadway. Autumn set her down and she and Hoot stood careful guard.

"Where are we heading?" I asked my husband.

"North for now. Away from the ash."

I looked to the south. Mt. Rainier was still releasing a stream of smoke and volcanic material. It was farther away and appeared much smaller, but still made me nervous.

"There's no point in heading back south. Anything near the mountain will be covered in volcanic spew and flooded from the melted glaciers."

"Someplace new, then," I said quietly.

"Graeme wants to head to Canada. He says he heard a brief radio transmission a few months back about a safe zone on Vancouver Island. I don't think we have much choice. We need to check it out."

"Graeme - is that the guy who's driving the bus?" I asked.

"Yeah. He's a good guy. Doesn't talk much. He lost his family when this all started."

I didn't ask how. Questions like that were typically best left unasked. If we were lucky, there would be time to get to know him later.

"Canada it is, then."

"Hope's acting weird," he said quietly.

"She won't let me touch her. Maybe she's just exhausted."

"Probably scared too. Let's go. I don't like it here," he admitted. "It's too open."

"I haven't been able to feel them for a while. Or you."

"You're not pregnant, right?"

"We haven't exactly done it lately," I grumbled.

"We'll change that as soon as we get settled. I promise."

He bent down slightly and kissed me gently on my lips. I wish I could say I felt an electric charge, but my extra sense

108

seemed dead. Instead I inhaled as I took in the warmth of his lips and the softness of his short beard.

Graeme stepped up onto a small boulder that sat just a couple of feet off the highway and clapped his hands only loud enough to catch the attention of those of us still outside the bus. Within a couple of seconds, we all fell silent in anticipation of whatever it was he wanted to say.

He began by clearing his throat gently. "I want to get back on the road in just a minute. We've had a few injuries and the engine on the bus is acting up. It's probably just clogged from all the ash, but as soon as we come across some other options we'll need to ditch this beast. The plan for now is to keep heading north and cross the border into Canada."

"That's one big place," said a short man with graying hair and a thick neck. "What do you hope to find there?"

"Last radio transmission I got mentioned a safe zone on Vancouver Island. And, to be honest, I don't know where else to go."

"The kids need to eat," said Autumn.

"Flower eat too!" chirped Hope.

As if hearing her name, the little dog erupted from the front door of the bus and ran out into the field beside us. Her bark was high pitched and angry and her hackles were up. Her shrill yipping turned to a mixture of growling and whining as her tail drooped down between her hind legs.

"Everyone back on the bus!" said Gus between clench teeth.

"What is it?" asked Hoot.

"The dead. I can feel them nearby," Gus said as he placed a hand over his heart and massaged. "Get on board, now! Start the engine…"

I rushed toward Autumn, Hoot, and Hope. I was closer to the door of the bus. Hoot took Hope from Autumn's arms, took the woman's hand in his, and began to run. I held my arms out to take my daughter, but she refused. As soon as she was planted into my arms, bitter cold fell over my arms and chest. It felt like the grip of an icy fist, at first starting with a frosty burn that grew quickly to an electric-like shock. I clenched Hope with my hands, determined to get her up the steps and behind the safety of the sheet metal and barred windows of the converted bus. The hands that I so desperately tried to use to cling to my daughter failed me, the burning sensation causing me to let go. As Hope slid down my front I couldn't understand why she didn't try to hold onto me. She landed at the top of the steps with a small thud and looked up at me. Her pale face was wet with tears, her nose running.

She began sobbing, to a point of being nearly unintelligible. "Mama no touch! Mama no touch me! Mama no!"

I could feel my heart struggling to beat within my chest while my lungs painfully fought to take in air. Standing became too difficult and while I wanted to reach forward toward my little girl, I instead fell backward. My vision blurred as I hit the hard ground at the bottom of the bus steps. Ringing in my ears distorted the voice calling my name, but I knew it was Gus. Everything felt cold. The ground. Gus' hands. The air that refused to enter my chest.

"Hoot, get Hope out of here! Zoe, don't you dare die on me, darlin'!"

My throat made a strange high pitched noise that sounded nothing like it came from a human being. I opened my eyes wide and focused on Gus' panicked face while my back arched painfully. I kept my eyes open, not by choice, and my vision began to fade. Unable to draw a breath, the last thing I saw before things went black was Gus raising his fist above me. His fist striking my chest caused excruciating pain. The air that flooded my lungs burned intensely. Hope's screaming in the distance was worse than the torture my body felt. Soon many people were screaming around me. I gasped for breath, writhing on the ground. The smell of death burned my nose when I was able to finally inhale. Gus was no longer at my side and my hip ached deeply. The sound of a shotgun pierced my left ear and the smell of gunpowder mingled with that of decay. The sounds of the dead mixed with that of men and women yelling, the dog barking, and muffled screaming from somewhere within the bus. Arms encircled me and pulled me to a standing position.

My head was still filled with fog and my heart beat was uncomfortably irregular as if threatening to stall altogether.

"C'mon, friend," said the woman holding onto me. "Inside!"

I struggled to cling to her as she eagerly encouraged me up the steps of the bus. Hope's cries intensified once I was aboard. I searched for her frantically. She sounded like she was in pain. I found her in the back of the bus on one of the couches, Hoot and Autumn holding onto her while she writhed.

"Hope," I croaked out.

My voice sent her into a frenzy. I wasn't sure if she was scared for me, or of me. She all but climbed behind Autumn. Hoot stood and coughed.

"Jessa, bring her back here to the couch!"

The woman supporting me, Jessa, didn't answer but began walking toward the longest of the two couches. Hoot threw a blanket down, presumably to cover vomit from the woman who had been there at the start of the trip. Gunfire continued outside. I was sure I heard Gus screaming at someone. Once to the edge of the couch, I toppled onto it. My knees instinctively drew toward my chest and my arms crossed each other. I was so cold it hurt from head to toe.

"Mommy," moaned Hope. "Mommy…I sorry, Mama!"

The bus rocked heavily as more of the group piled onboard.

"Where is she?" boomed Gus' voice. "Zoe!"

"She's back here," said Hoot loudly.

My teeth chattered and I clenched my eyes closed. I felt like I had chugged a Slurpee and had the worst brain freeze possible. Gus' hands embraced my face. They were so warm they almost burned.

"Zoe, what happened?" he asked, his voice stern yet caring.

I blinked, but found myself unable to keep my eyes open.

"Look at me, baby," he said. The alarm in his voice was frightening.

I forced my eyes open but was unable to focus on his face.

"H-h-hope," I stammered, fighting the tremble of my jaw.

"She's here, baby. Hoot has her."

I struggled to clear my vision, but was unable to see past his face.

"Gus," interrupted Hoot.

"What?" he asked, still not looking away from me.

"You need to see this," he said. His voice sounded grim.

"Go-g-go," I said through chattering teeth.

"Jessa, can you cover her up?" asked my husband.

"On it," said the woman. "Jenny, can you bring one of the afghans? And some hand warmers?"

I closed my eyes and focused on breathing. My chest still burned with the need for oxygen. Jenny and Jessa opened the instant hand warmers and soon they were tucked under my arms, in my hands, at my groin, and the base of my neck. Hoot and Gus spoke in hushed tones, but I knew by the tone of Gus' voice he was both angry and fearful.

"Hope, come to me right now," he said, trying to force our daughter to leave Autumn's arms.

I had never heard him speak to her that harshly before. Her crying instantly intensified.

"Hope!" he shouted.

"G-g-gus…no," I groaned.

"Gus, the skin on her arms is black. Look," interrupted Autumn.

"It hurts, dada!" Hope whimpered pathetically.

I struggled to sit up, but Jessa held a hand on my shoulder.

"Hope?" I called out. "Baby what's wrong?"

"Mama we hurt!" her crying got louder.

"Gus, bring her to me," I begged.

She began screaming. "No! No Mama! No no no!"

"Jessa, let me up!" I used one of my hands to shoo her away from me

As soon as I was on my feet, the bus lurched forward and I fell backwards, landing on my butt. Gus got to Hope well before I could and knelt in front of her on the couch. He reached for her despite her look of horror and screeches of protest. The sounds of distress coming from my daughter made me sick to my stomach.

"Gus, don't touch her," I said loudly.

"Fuck, Zoe, we need to see what's wrong!" he snapped at me and tried to take Hope out of Autumn's arms.

Blood ran down Autumn's face as Hope clawed at her. She immediately let go of our daughter and Gus used the opportunity to bring her to him, holding her tightly against his chest while steadying her head with his chin. She hit, kicked, and clawed until he let go. I knew something was very wrong when Hoot pulled her back and her arms and cheek were black with skin sloughing off in sheets.

"Hope…" I cried out.

She wailed from pain as Gus struggled to catch his breath. The left side of his beard looked wet and as I knelt to inspect him, I could see it was bloody fluid. I looked at Hope, who looked back at me with fear and tears in her eyes.

"Let me take her till we figure it out," said Hoot with unusual calmness.

Gus rubbed at his chin and stared at Hope. I could tell he was worried about Hope, confused, and frustrated. He quickly pulled his hand away from his face.

"She burnt me," he whispered as he looked at the fluid left behind on his fingertips. "Hope, baby, what's happening?" he asked her.

She clung to Hoot and sobbed.

"She's in pain," said Hoot. "Can we give her an aspirin or something?"

"Never aspirin for kids," Gus mumbled. "Give her a quarter of a Tylenol."

"Gus, what's wrong with her?" It seemed a stupid question, but I wasn't sure what else to say.

"Autumn, are you okay?" asked Hoot.

"I will be, but she really got my forehead. I should clean it."

"I'll help," said Jenny. It wasn't until she spoke that I realized the bus load of people had been quiet during the odd display.

Hope's cries began to subside. Hoot held her close and rubbed her back gently. I could see her small body twitch on occasion, a sure sign that she was falling asleep.

"Her arms," I said. I could hear the distress in my own voice. "What's wrong with her arms?"

Gus ignored me and focused his attention onto Hoot. "Once she's asleep lay her on the couch, brother?"

Finally, Gus scooted toward me. "I'm not sure what's wrong, but I'll look at her once she's asleep."

"She sounds like she's in so much pain," I said as I wiped a tear from my cheek. Knowing my baby was hurting was agonizing.

Hoot cleared his throat gently as he stood with Hope in his arms. Her left arm hung limply, the dark area spreading well past her elbow and threatening to encompass her chubby little hand. Her pale curls were plastered to her cheek and forehead from perspiration. My worry grew by the minute.

Still wrapped in a blanket, I stood to make room for Hope on the couch. When Hoot set her down, she whimpered in her sleep.

"Gus, do something," I said with a trembling voice.

"She looks horrible," I whispered to my husband, not wanting Hope to hear, even in her sleep.

"I know. Let me look her over, okay?"

I nodded. My chest still felt tight where my daughter had rested her head. I scooted aside to give Gus access to her small body. He reached for her arm.

"No," said the woman named Jessa. "Don't touch her. Let me."

She wedged herself between Gus and the couch.

"Jessa, what is it?" I asked as I watched her inspect Hope's arm.

"She's burnt. Badly. Someone get me the first aid kit," she snapped.

The bus lurched forward, causing me to fall sideway against the couch. Hope cried out, disturbed by the motion. As I

114

steadied myself and focused on her as she slept fitfully, I could see the skin of her wrist darkening.

She began gasping for breath and her body stiffened. Her tiny hands curled into fists so tight that her knuckles paled. Her left leg began jerking first, quickly followed by her left arm. Gus reached for her. Before Jessa could block him, his hand touched her left thigh. He pulled his hand away quickly, cursing under his breath.

"Let me," barked Jessa.

"She's having a seizure," said a man sitting nearby. "My brother used to have them when we were kids. Looked just like that."

"Don't try to hold her still. Just keep her from rolling off the couch," Gus directed through a shaky voice.

"Jenny, I need your help," called Jessa.

I hesitantly scooted farther away from my daughter, knowing that Jenny would need the space.

"She's hot," whispered Jessa as Jenny knelt beside her.

"How long has she been seizing?" asked Jenny.

"Not long. Maybe twenty seconds?"

I covered my mouth with my hand when Hope began making unintelligible noises. Her jaw was clenched shut and her breathing sounded wet. Her entire hand was black, even where her knuckles had paled from her tight grip. Her thigh bore a bright red mark in the shape of Gus' palm. The edges were already turning black. Time seemed to stand still as her spasms finally subsided. She remained on her side, lying limp with phlegm audibly dancing in her windpipe. Jenny and Jessa skillfully turned her to her other side to face them. Jessa used the corner of a nearby blanket to rid Hope's mouth of mucus.

"Is she okay? Why isn't she waking up?" I asked, barely above a whisper.

The bus swayed as the driver hit potholes in the road.

"She just had a seizure," said Jenny softly. "Most people will sleep pretty hard afterward. It's like her body just ran a marathon and her energy got all used up."

"Jessa," said Gus firmly.

"I see it," she replied.

Hope's arm worsened to the point of skin sloughing off, exposing muscle and bone. Jessa gently took hold of her hand to inspect the wound. Hope cried out but never opened her eyes. She took a shuddering breath before the stillness of death claimed her.

Gus made a noise in his throat. He choked it back and calmed himself while Jennie turned her attention back to our daughter.

"Hand me that blanket," she said softly.

The two women worked together to gently cover Hope, head to toe.

"I want to hold her," I said pleadingly.

"I don't think that's a good idea," said Hoot from behind us.

"Please," I begged as I lost composure. "Just let me hold her one more time."

Gus wrapped his arms around me and buried his head against the curve between my shoulder and neck. "I'm so sorry, Zoe," he sobbed. I felt his warm tears trickle down my neck.

"Not again," I moaned.

My eyes filled with tears as I looked at the still form of our beloved daughter. She was our Hope, in more ways than one. She held the secrets that could save humanity. She lay there so small and so motionless.

"What happened?" choked Autumn.

"Gus, do something," I pleaded.

"She's gone, baby. She's gone." Gus' words were filled with the strain of disbelief and shock. They were unusually void of emotion; hollow.

"No!" I screamed. "Hope, wake up!"

I was vaguely aware of sobbing in the background. Gus held me firmly while I struggled to reach for my baby. I needed to be with her, to stroke her white curls and kiss her forehead and whisper to her one last time "mama loves you."

A pain filled my chest that I knew all too well. It wasn't the cold grip around my heart that tried to claim me only minutes earlier. It was a memory from what seemed like a lifetime ago. The pain of losing Molly shortly after her birth had dulled as time went on, but at that moment it came back and hit me ten-fold. It was joined by the agony I felt when I had found little Emmett killed and reanimated and had been burdened with the task of driving a blade into the base of his still-soft baby skull. The loss of Emilie, Boggs, Louisa, little Jane. Each heartache compounded the ones before.

"Let me hold her," I demanded.

"Darlin', it's not safe," Gus said, trying to calm me. "I can't lose you too."

"Let me die!" I shouted. "Let me go with her!"

"Shhh," he soothed. "Always choose life, baby. I can't let you go with her."

I cried into his shoulder. My heart felt void of life, as if each beat was for no reason.

CHAPTER 13

A mile later, or maybe a hundred, the bus came to a rolling stop. Hoot took over restraining me when I couldn't stand Gus' touch anymore. Gus hadn't tried to save her. No one had. No CPR, no rescue breathing. Nothing. I pleaded with him to save my Molly, and I pleaded with him to save Hope, and he did nothing to help either of them.

"That's it, folks. End of the line. Bus is dead, probably from the ash mucking up the lines," said Graeme the driver. He stood to face us all.

Gus also stood. I refused to look up at him.

"We need to bury my daughter."

Gus' voice lacked emotion.

"Where are we?" asked the woman from earlier who had vomited all over herself.

"I figure somewhere south of the border. I haven't seen a sign in a while, but I think we're somewhere in the Methow Valley. I used to ride my bike through here every damn summer, but it's so overgrown I just can't be sure," Said Graeme.

It was the most I had heard the man say at once. I didn't care what he had to say. I didn't care where we were, or where we were going. We were broken down in the middle of nowhere and my daughter was lying four feet away from me no longer living. Jessa sat near her head with a blade in hand.

"Gus, we need to leave as soon as possible. I'll step out with Diego and get the ground ready," said Graeme.

"No. It needs to be me," said Gus.

"That's fine," said a man near Gus in age.

I hadn't taken notice of him until then. He reminded me of a blonde version of Boggs. The reminder only caused my heart to break a little bit more.

"But let us help. Time is never on our side."

Gus grunted his acceptance. He turned to face me. While I refused to look at his face, I could tell that he wanted to say something to me. Instead he addressed Hoot.

"Can you take her to the front of the bus? Or outside? While I take care of Hope?"

Hoot's arms tightened around me as my entire body tensed.

"No!" I screamed loudly. "No! Don't touch her!"

My own voice was shrill and filled with panic. I knew my mouth had opened and I had made a noise, but was it really me who screamed so pathetically? Surely not. They were going to hurt her. They were going to cut her and destroy her brain.

"Hoot!" yelled Gus angrily.

I continued to cry out while Hoot forced me to my feet and lifted me in his arms.

"She has to be quiet!" said a short woman with tight dark curls. "They'll hear her!"

"Fuck you!" I spat at the woman as Hoot carried me past her. "Fuck all of you!"

As we descended the stairs near the driver's seat, I stop fighting Hoot and crumpled in his arms.

"Shhh," he soothed quietly. "I'm here, Zoe."

The fresh air hit me as we left the shelter of the bus, perhaps because it lacked the stench of death to which we were now accustomed. It made reality seem even more tangible and the fury of knowing they were driving a knife into my little girl's brain enraged me. I thrashed in Hoot's arms, but he took his responsibility seriously and didn't let go.

Footfalls came toward us and I stilled.

"Gus, let me help Graeme with the grave," said Hoot. "You need to be with Zoe right now."

"Thanks, brother."

Gus spoke with a tightness in his throat and the congestion of tears lacing his words. I didn't want him to touch me, but when Hoot transferred me to my husband's arms I unexpectedly melted into him and cried against his chest. He stroked my hair and cried with me. He pulled me to the ground where he held me on his lap. The sound of shovels scarring the earth grated on each of my raw nerves. Gus leaned against the bus and I leaned against him. Hope was wrapped in a blanket when Autumn carried her from the bus to the new gaping hole in the ground. We were both too broken to stand. I couldn't bear watching her lowered into the ground or to witness the dirt being shoveled on top of her. My memories of burying Molly mingled with what I knew was happening to my precious Hope. I kept my eyes in the opposite direction and focused on a layer of gray clouds in the distance.

"There's no ash here," I whispered only loud enough for Gus to hear.

My throat was raw from screaming. I wasn't sure he had understood what I said.

"No ash," he echoed. "Just fresh air and a beautiful view."

"I can't keep doing this."

"I know. I'll do it for both of us right now."

"I want to stay here with her. The dead can come and take me. Just leave me here," I said quietly begging.

"Always choose life. It's just me and you. We'll get through this."

He had lost so much more than I. His two children of the world. Molly. Emmett. Now Hope. How could he bear it? How could he not agree to just let me go?

"She can't really be gone. How did this happen?" I began sobbing. "How?"

"I don't have answers."

He stroked my hair more firmly and kissed the top of my head. His hand trembled and in that moment I knew he needed me as much as I did him. The high pitched screech of a hawk sounded overhead. I looked up and watched as it teetered side to side in the wind, circling. When it dove to the earth to catch its prey, my eyes didn't follow. Rather, I stared off in the distance wishing I could wake up from the nightmare happening around us. I tried to tune out the sound of dirt being tossed on my daughter's body. Eventually I closed my eyes and allowed my body to go limp in Gus' arms. I forced my breathing to slow and focused on listening for his slow heartbeat. Time was in the background and passed whether we wanted it to or not.

"Okay, people! Listen up!" boomed Graeme's voice.

Gus shifted beneath me and I took a shuddering breath inward.

"We need to move. Grab what you can and we'll follow the highway north till we find a new rig or shelter. If we're where I think we are we'll come across a small town called Burn in ten or fifteen miles. Stay alert. If you have a gun keep it readied. If you don't, make sure you have a knife or something to hit them with. We leave in five."

Sam approached us and held his good arm out for me. I looked at him just stared.

"C'mon, let me help you," he said.

I didn't want to get up and I didn't want to go anywhere, but my body betrayed me by taking his hand and standing. I felt numb and trapped and on the verge of panic. Gus' boots dragged in the loose gravel and dirt that had collected on the roadway. I turned to face him and we took each other's hands. He leaned down far enough to touch his forehead to mine. I couldn't feel his soul at all anymore, but I knew from his lack of energy and erratic breathing pattern that he was exhausted.

"We have to go," he whispered.

"I know."

***

As Graeme had hoped, we came upon the town of Burn after about six hours. We kept a brisk pace to avoid lingering in one place for too long. Our longest rest break was never more than five minutes. There were no useful vehicles on our path. We saw Roamers sporadically. Any that were close enough to worry about were taken out by those with knives or blunt objects.

We lost several more people at the rest stop we had taken when Hope's touch had caused me to collapse. The dead had closed in on the bus and not everyone made it back aboard. Flower the little dog was amongst those who died. I hadn't known our fallen comrades, but Sam told me a little boy who was about five years old and a teenage girl had been amongst them. The woman covered in vomit was also gone. I tried to keep my mind blank, but losing Hope filled my head constantly. I was barely aware when the small town came to view. Gus took my hand and we continued toward two small buildings on the left. They were both boarded up and weathered.

"Doesn't look like anyone's been here in a long time," said Jessa quietly.

"I don't want to mess with these buildings just yet. They look too ragged to be secured. Let's keep going and see what's ahead," said Graeme.

"Everyone stay alert," said Gus.

The highway curved to the right for about the length of a football field. When we finally got to the end the earth banked sharply to the right and on the left sat a small one-story brick building in the shape of an "L." A sign out front read *Maryweather Assisted Living & Senior Daycare*.

"We should scope it out," said Gus.

"I agree," said Jenny. "It'll be dark soon."

"If we're lucky it was evacuated before the world went to shit," interjected Jessa. "Jenny and I can scope out any med carts for usable things. We'll know what to look for."

"I can help," said Gus.

"Gus was a nurse too," Hoot said to Jessa, who nodded in acknowledgement.

"Worst case scenario, the place is infested. We'll have to judge if it's worth trying to salvage anything once we're inside. Looks like there's two main wings, so I suggest we clear it in teams of four," said Graeme.

"I may not be the best shot with just one hand, so I should pass my gun off to someone else," said Sam.

"Jessa and Jenny you two go with Graeme and Autumn. Hoot, I want you with me and Zoe and Sam," said Gus matter-of-factly.

"You got it," our friend replied briskly.

"Priority is to put down anything we find to be a risk. We can clear bodies later. Jenny and Jess, once we've rid the place of the dead you can search the med carts to your hearts content," said Graeme.

He and Gus seemed to flow seamlessly as co-leaders.

"Zo, are you gonna be okay to do this?" Gus whispered to me.

I looked up at him somewhat blankly. "Yeah. I'm just not quite here right now."

"That's what worries me. Stay alert, darlin', and focus on not getting hurt. We'll mourn together soon."

I took a deep breath and gripped my knife tightly before taking a step forward. I suddenly didn't care if the dead might be waiting to devour me. I could no longer sense them, or Gus. Hope's silent words no longer reflected as emotions within my mind. Everyone I had ever loved, aside from Gus, was gone. Life was hardly worth living.

The other team headed toward the larger of the two wings as the rest of us proceeded to a set of double glass entry doors. The panes were coated in months, if not years, of dust and grime. I held my trusted hammer at my right side and took a position just in front of Sam, who carried a piece of pipe he scavenged. Both of us were still nursing arm injures so left the guns to Hoot and Gus, figuring our aim would be better with blunt weapons.

I used the back of my good hand, still clutching the hammer, to wipe away a small area of dirt from the pane of glass.

"Look, the inside is painted black," I whispered.

"Ayup," said Gus. "Probably someone tried to hole up here. Be alert in case they're still here."

"Alive or dead," contributed Sam.

"Stay back a few feet while I open her up," said Hoot. "Gus, cover me?"

"You got it, brother."

The handles on the doors were typical metal pulls than ran vertically. Gus pulled on one, opening the door. From the looks on my companions faces, none of us expected them to be unlocked. Hoot covered his mouth and nose when the smell hit him. Gus held his rifle up and waited. When nothing emerged to consume us, he nodded and stepped into the darkness. Sam followed while Hoot kept the door ajar. I stepped in next. The entry was dark, lit only by the light that crept in with us. Gus turned on a flashlight. Cobwebs hung wherever they had been able to take root. Dust coated black vinyl chairs and couches. There was a small office and greeting counter to our left. A vase of flowers was only recognizable by stems that had dried long ago. Papers were strewn about and a computer tower and monitor were laying on the floor, electrical bits and glass broken and scattered about. How the vase of dead flowers had survived intact was a mystery.

"There," whispered Sam.

I looked up and followed his line of sight. On the floor lay a body, halfway between the lobby and a smaller room. The torso was masked by the darkness, leaving only a pair of legs visible to us. Whoever it was had lost the skin from foot to knee, where it transitioned to mummification.

"Been here awhile," said Gus quietly.

"Let's go in a bit deeper," I suggested.

There was only one option: straight ahead. A hallway stood before us, dark and foreboding. As we began our trek into the darkness, Hoot clicked a pen light on. It caused shadows to dance in front of us. The effect was disorienting but being able to see to face dangers was critical. Doors lined the right hand side of the hallway. Each was shut. The other side of the hall was lined with floral prints in cheap frames and windows, all of which were painted black like the entry.

"We need to clear the rooms," said Gus.

"Let's start with the ones closest to the exit, and don't forget to keep an eye on the front door. We don't need any surprises," said Sam.

Gus poised himself to open the first door. Before he had a chance to open it, I spoke up.

"It'll go faster if we split into two teams. Hoot, I'll go with you. Sam, you can go with Gus."

"You don't want to stick with Gus?" asked Hoot.

"No. It's not that. I just know we're both distracted, so it's best if each of us teams up with someone who isn't."

Gus looked down at his boots. "She's right."

We didn't speak after that. We opened the first six doors without issue. The rooms each held three electric beds, still semi-dressed in white sheets and quilts and afghans. A few were bare as if waiting for a new patient to arrive. In one, an IV pole lay haphazardly in its side next to a bed that was smeared in feces that had long ago dried. Hoot and I had the pleasure of clearing that one. The seventh door led to the ladies' restroom. It held a single toilet and sink and one corner was dedicated to a walk-in shower. The toilet had clearly been used several times and now held a composted slush. I left the room quickly, gagging as I ran out.

Hoot and I took the last door, number nine, while Gus and Sam went back to shut the prior doors. As soon as Hoot pushed the door inward, the growling of the dead broke the silence we had until then enjoyed. We held back long enough for Hoot to sweep the room with the narrow beam of his pen light. The creature that sounded tortured was in the back corner. Male or female was a guess. It was sitting still strapped into a wheelchair, tipped onto its side. It was bloated, much like a Hunter, but postured and sounded like a Roamer. Thin gray hair plastered to stretched, moist-appearing skin on its forehead. It had no legs. A double amputee. Jaws opened and closed as it struggled to pull itself toward us.

"Jesus," said Hoot. "The poor fuck."

I walked to it, boldly.

"Zoe, I'll get it," said Hoot.

"No. Let me."

I held my knife tightly and squatted in front of the snapping jaws. I looked into the eyes of the creature. They were clouded and sunken. One pupil appeared silver, the other a hue of green. I sensed nothing from it, but knew it was ravenous. There was something else, though. Sadness. Its eyes held sadness. We fixed on each other and the creature's jaws stopped snapping at me. As my face drew nearer to that of the dead, everything around me grew silent. The air grew warm and filled with the scent of old lady roses and moth balls. A great sense of peace swirled around me and filled me. As I began to merge with the creature on some nonphysical level I couldn't begin to understand, the air was sucked from my lungs when I was torn from a plane of numbing bliss. My spine hit the edge of something hard, causing searing pain in my ribs. I struggled to breathe again while watching Hoot kick the creature's head until it split open and oozed black clots of rotting brain tissue onto the floor.

"Zoe!" he yelled as he ran back to me. "We have to go! Get up!"

I looked at him, not quite comprehending. There were too many noises around us. Yelling, gunfire, someone screaming. The crash of metal and breaking glass.

"Get her out!" I heard Gus shout.

"Jesus Christ! There's more coming!"

"The front door's blocked! Get out the windows!"

"They're out there too. Oh God, watch out!"

I recognized each voice but had trouble attaching them to their owners.

Hoot grabbed me forcefully under my bandaged arm. The resulting pain brought me out of my haze.

"Hoot! What is it?" I demanded, yelling to be heard over the commotion.

"Get up! We have to move!" was his only answer.

"Gus!" I screamed.

The only reply was rapid gunfire and screaming. Hoot pulled on my arm as I struggled to get away.

"Gus!" I yelled again.

"Zoe, get out!" he finally answered.

"Stop fighting me, damnit!" growled Hoot.

The gunfire stopped suddenly and my core filled with ice as a new scream pierced the air. The only times I had ever heard a scream that grating and full of pain was when someone was being consumed alive by the dead. It lasted far too long, finally being cut short by the sound of a single shot.

A vibration tore through the building. It was low and deep and vaguely familiar. My footing became unstable when the building lurched. Bits of dust and ceiling rained down around us and my ears were filled by a strange sensation akin to pressure.

"Duck and cover!" yelled Gus.

Hoot forced me to the ground and climbed on top of me. His weight was crushing. Another explosion rocked the building, but farther in the distance. The area quickly grew to be a mini war zone, littering us with debris. Hoot tightened his arms around me each time a new blast shook us. What must have only lasted a few minutes felt like an eternity. Eventually the explosions stopped and the moans of the dead and screams of the living and the sounds of gunfire faded, replaced by the creaking and moaning of an unstable building.

"Are you okay?" Hoot whispered against my cheek.

I wasn't able to find my voice, so nodded my head instead.

"Stay still while I try to stand up."

I nodded again.

He shifted his weight and took a sharp breath inward.

"Fuck," he groaned.

"What's wrong?" I whispered.

"I think something hit my ankle. It hurts like a bastard. I jarred my fucking wrist too. Son of a mother fuck."

The sound of rubble shifting in the distance caused us both worry. We weren't in a good position to fight or defend.

"Zoe? Hoot?"

Gus' voice. He was alive. I took a small breath of relief.

"Here," I called back. "Hoot's hurt."

"Stay there. I'll find you guys."

I froze when I heard unfamiliar voices. Someone was barking instructions. *Check for survivors. Make sure they're not human before you put them down. I saw eight enter and we've only got the one girl on board. One's dead. Looking for six more.*

Hoot and I hunkered down waiting for Gus. He found us quickly and with not much effort.

"Did you guys hear that?" asked Gus in a very low whisper.

"Yeah," Hoot and I said in unison.

"I think we need to risk it," Hoot said to Gus in particular.

"I don't trust people anymore," Gus admitted. "But, your foot looks fucked up and we need to get to safety."

The two men nodded at each other before looking at me. I nodded my agreement.

"We're here to help!" called a deep male voice.

"Call out if you can hear us," a much softer feminine voice called out.

"Here! We're here!" I called out.

"How many?" the woman called back.

"Three," I yelled.

"Stay put. We'll come to you."

I began to shake as adrenaline continued to build in my system.

CHAPTER 14

The reconnaissance group found us while on one of their final scouting missions; they were on their way back to what they called Alpha Base. Their diesel fuel supply was running critically low, and they were desperate to fill their large trucks with supplies before running out. The horde rushing the old folk's home was a sure sign of life inside. Chanel, the woman who had ultimately located us was young and had a kind face. Her dark brown hair was cropped short on one side and fell to her chin on the other. There were five in her group in all, but three were lost when the dead overtook them just outside the nursing home. As I suspected, Graeme was gone. It was Jessa who fired the shot that ended his torture. She hadn't spoken since and Gus explained that she was in shock. Sam survived, but barely. A wall collapsed near him, re-shattering his injured wrist. Jenny hadn't been as fortunate. She was killed in one of the blasts. We searched for Autumn until a new wave of the dead approached. We never did find her, alive or dead, leaving morale low.

The vehicle we were in was a piecemeal of different automobiles. The cab from a pickup, the body of a large windowless van. A hatch was welded into the ceiling with a metal platform bolted to the floor below and bench seats lined the inside walls. Holes no larger than two inches in diameter were drilled at even spaces about two feet below ceiling height. Chanel sat in the back with us while her companion took the front driver's seat. He was an older man who bore scars on his left arm and face, and I suspected he bore a lot of mental baggage. He didn't say much, but when he did his voice was commanding if not terrifying. Hoot sat beside Jessa, trying to comfort her. Sam lay on the rear-most bench, thankfully not conscious. His hand was bloody and unnaturally twisted. It was beginning to turn purple from swelling. Even in his deep sleep, an occasional wince or moan escaped him.

"Chanel, I need you up top! There's one of the fast ones at 11o'clock," the man said gruffly.

"On top of it," she called back.

She stepped up onto the metal platform and struggled to push the hatch open. She was clearly too short to be effective with the task. Gus stood and jumped into action, helping her.

"Let me get it," he said in a cool and even tone.

"Chanel! I've got a bad feeling!" called the driver.

"Ernie, I can't reach! I'm sending the new guy up top!"

"Zoe, hand me your pistol!" Gus shouted down to me.

The metal hatch made a loud thud on the roof of the van as it slammed backward. Gus disappeared from the waist up and I handed him my gun. Before long the sound of shooting was followed by Ernie emitting a loud "whoop!"

Four more pops came from the gun and the van swerved to the left.

"Bring him back down, Chanel. We're clear enough."

"On it."

"I'll get him," I said as I stood.

Sam began moaning in the background. Chanel looked at me and nodded.

"I'll tend to your friend. What's his name?"

"Sam," I said quickly. "His wrist was already broken, but not like this."

"We have a first aid kit. I'll give him a shot of morphine. Once we get home we'll have Doc look at him."

I tugged at Gus' jeans to signal him down. The van-slash-truck jarred to the left and I stumbled, catching myself against Gus as he emerged from the hatch.

"Careful," he said as we struggled to upright ourselves.

Sam yelped in pain.

"Ernie, what the hell is going on?" Chanel called up to the cab.

"Fucking animal or something ran across the road. I got it." The jolting calmed as he straightened the vehicle.

"Or something?" asked Hoot.

"Not sure what it was. It's almost dusk," answered the driver. "I don't wanna turn around to find out."

"Yeah, sounds good," said Hoot. His forehead was wrinkled and he looked full of deep thought.

"Sam? My name's Chanel. I'm gonna stick you with some morphine, love, okay?"

His teeth were clenched and his brow was soaked in sweat. The best he was able to do was groan between his teeth.

"Chanel, do you need help with that?" asked Gus.

"I've almost got it." She struggled to stick the syringe needle into a small vial. The routine motion of the vehicle made it difficult and she unfortunately stuck herself in the hand.

Gus crouched down beside her and took the vial.

"I'm used to doing this on the move. I'll take over if it's okay?"

"Yeah sure," she answered. "Are you a doctor?"

"Former ARMY nurse. Humvee, helicopter, boat...you name it, I've delivered care in pretty rough terrain."

I sat on the remaining bench seat and watched Gus work. Chanel stayed at his side to help hold Sam's arm still. She seemed eager to learn and eager to help others. Something about her was calming. It was a matter of only seconds after Gus injected the medication into Sam's vein that he calmed. Chanel covered him with a yellow blanket as he fell asleep. Gus rummaged through the first aid kit while Chanel excused herself to sit up front with Ernie.

As she walked past me, I stood and caught her attention.

"Thanks for helping Sam."

"It's no problem. Really."

She smiled at me. Her eyes were a warm chocolate brown. We had encountered so many evil people on our journey so far that it was difficult to trust anyone new. Chanel felt different.

"Nell, I'm pulling off at the next clearing," said Ernie.

"I hate it when he calls me that," she grumbled before flashing a brief smile at me. "Okay. Want me to drive the rest of the way?"

"You know it," he said with a sigh.

"I better head up front. We'll talk more later," she said.

I sat back down on the bench seat and drew my knees to my chest and buried my face in my arms. My forearm ached and I felt dizzy. My heart ached for both of my daughters, as well as baby Emmett. For a moment I considered using the morphine in the first aid kit for myself, a dose big enough to end my own life. Shortly after, Gus sat down next to me. I kept my face down. He exhaled loudly and wrapped his arms around me hard.

"No, Zoe. We've both lost so much. I can't lose you too."

He had heard me, even though his spirit was absent within my own mind; yet another void in my life.

I cried softly and leaned against him, still not looking up.

"It hurts so bad," I moaned. "I can't live without her, Gus. I can't."

"We have to, love. Hope would want us to live. Anything less would be dishonoring her beautiful memory."

I finally lifted my head. Gus used his thumbs to wipe the tears that were streaming down my face.

"How am I supposed to go on, though?" I asked quietly.

"Our love for each other, darlin'. Right now it's all I have to give you. It has to be enough. Let it be enough. Please, let it be enough?"

I clung to him, the pain from my gunshot wound paling in comparison to the pain within my heart. Eventually the vehicle slowed and came to a stop.

"We're taking a quick rest break," Gus said as he kissed the top of my head. "Do you need to get out?"

I shook my head side to side. "No."

"Lay down and sleep? Please?"

"'Kay. Just for a little while."

He stood and I allowed myself to stretch out horizontally. Gus tucked his jacket under my head and I soon fell into a fitful sleep. I woke briefly when Sam called out in pain, and again when Ernie fell into a coughing fit. Each time, Gus was sitting on the floor of the vehicle right beside me. Dreams came in bursts, each containing their own horrors: the dead devouring Hope's body, Molly in a crib crying for me, finding Gus dead in bed, being trapped in a car submerged in a river. Gus woke me from the worst of them; I had been dreaming that I died and came back as one of the living dead. In the nightmare, I had been about to devour Gus. It was a relief when my husband woke me.

"Chanel says we're almost there," he said to me. "They have a proper doctor who will look you and Sam over. I'll ask them for something to help you sleep."

"Where are we going?"

"They have a building they've secured up by the border. Some hole-in-the wall place that was under construction. Ernie says it's fortified and they're almost done finishing the exterior. They have about thirty people living there. He says it's secure, they have food, and medicine. I feel good about these people, Zo. I really do"

I nodded but didn't say anything.

The vehicle slowed and the brakes squealed as we went over a bump. Sam moaned but didn't wake up. He looked so pale and waxy. The bandage around his wrist was soaked in red.

"We're here," Chanel called back.

Ernie sat on the couch across from us. He stood, guarding his back like it ached.

"It'll just take the fence crew a minute to let us in," he said.

"How can we help?" asked Hoot.

"Just keep an eye out for the dead. We'll drive in and the crew will shut the gate behind us. We'll get your friend here to see Doc right away. Maybe help get him out of the van?"

"Sure. Anything."

134

After only a few moments the van proceeded forward at barely a crawl. Metal clanged as we drove over something. We all leaned as Chanel made a sharp right turn. We came to a stop and the engine died. Looking through one of the holes in the van wall, it looked like an underground parking garage.

"We're here," said Ernie with a stern look on his face. "I'll introduce you formally later, first I need to tell the rest of our group about our fallen comrades."

The barn doors on the back of the van opened and a short middle aged woman looked in. She wore a look of confusion.

"Ernie, you brought us survivors?"

"Yes, ma'am. One needs Doc real bad. Can you call for him?"

"Of course. Where's Barry, Caroline, and Ashok?"

Ernie shook his head side to side.

"Oh crap. Crap crap crap," she repeated. "That's gonna devastate the group."

Chanel made her way to the back of the rig and spoke softly. "Our new friends also lost a lot of their people."

"Well double crap," said the woman. "I'm real sorry to hear that."

She was a funny looking lady with thick coke-bottle glasses and wiry hair that fell just short of her shoulders. The ends were black, the rest silver. She seemed sincere and very comfortable in her own skin. She wore a black sweater that was big enough for her to swim in and pulled a walkie-talkie out from somewhere within its depths.

"Doc, you there?"

The hand held device crackled as she let go of the button and waited for a response.

"Doc, come in," she said.

Still no reply, she sighed heavily.

"Damn fruitcake is probably off sitting on the crapper again. He goes in there just to read. He doesn't think anyone is on to him."

She looked at her walkie and scowled at it.

"Doc, answer your call. We have someone down in the parking garage who's injured. Get your ass down here STAT."

The device cracked again, but was cut off by a deep voice.

"For Christ sake Olga, I'm coming."

She looked at us and smiled awkwardly.

"I'm Olga. Let's get you all inside."

Hoot spoke first. "I'll stay here to help with Sam. You guys go ahead and I'll meet up with you later."

The thought of splitting up didn't sit well with me. From his posture beside me, I could tell that Gus felt the same.

"We'd rather stick behind until we're sure Sam's okay," said Gus.

"Oh geez," interjected Olga. "We're not evil and your friend will be fine. Doc will be down and Ernie can help. Chanel, you can come up with us and break the news to the rest of our group. Damn shame we lost those three," she grumbled. "They were all real good people."

Olga said what she felt and certainly didn't sugar coat anything.

"Let's go," I said to Gus. "No offense, Olga, but we'd feel better if Hoot stays with our friend."

"Suit yourself," she said with a bit of a sigh as she turned and began to walk away. "Follow me."

Gus took my hand and gave it a gentle squeeze. We followed the quirky woman across a short expanse to a concrete stairwell. Several vehicles remained parked along one side of what was clearly a sub-level parking garage. Gaps in the concrete walls were reinforced with wire fencing. Wild plants sent roots in through cracks, attempting to lay claim to the structure. We ascended a short set of stairs and ran into a man who looked as quirky as Olga as we got to the first landing.

"Oh, hi," he said with an oddly chipper voice. "You must be our new friends. I'm Doc."

Gus held his hand out politely. "Gus. This is my wife, Zoe."

The man pumped Gus' hand enthusiastically.

136

"Nice to meet you both. Olga and Chanel will take good care of you but I must be off to help your friend. What's his name?" he asked as he turned to Olga.

"Sam. He looks pretty banged up."

Gus cleared his throat. "Sam has serious wrist injuries; it's been crushed twice.

"Right-o then. Off with ya."

As Olga turned to continue up the stairs, the man slapped her playfully on the butt before continuing on his way. She grumbled something unintelligible. I glanced at Gus, who winked at me. The gesture was out of place, not matching the graveness etched on his face. I knew his thoughts and heart were buried beside the road a long way behind us. I knew because mine were too.

"Olga, can you get these two to one of the empty units? I'll gather the others in the meeting hall to tell them about the others. Let them get settled and we'll make introductions over dinner."

"Yeah, yeah, no problem. Want me to set them up on the north or west side?"

"I think Dill wants to fill the north side first. There's four empty units."

"Alrighty then. Follow me," she said with a wave of her hand.

The door at the top of the stairwell was like any generic metal door of any generic building's stairwell. Metal painted dark brown with the number "2" on a small plaque.

"What is this building?" asked Gus.

"It was going to be shops below and apartments up top. It was still under construction so the units above us aren't finished. They work, though. We're slowly finishing off the living spaces and we've converted most of the office spaces into open areas for social stuff. Meetings. Game night. A movie once a week. The foundation was already in and we just had to close off the open areas in the garage with wire fencing and clear the office spaces of the dead. Luckily it was a weekend when this shit happened so not many people had been here. Just the janitorial night crew of three. One got caught outside when the shit hit the fan. Got back inside before it died and came back"

We continued up the stairs with Olga in the lead while Chanel branched off.

"Bridgid was the only one who survived. She managed to hide in the air duct for a few days. When we found her she was near death from dehydration. It took her weeks to recover, mostly emotionally," explained Chanel. "You'll like her. She's really funny if you can get her to loosen up."

"This is the first floor, of four. The top two we're using for storage. Food, necessities. The roof has a garden for smaller things. Tomatoes, herbs, stuff that's easy. We've expanded behind the building. There's cargo containers around the perimeter with a large garden and a small orchard. Well, the trees are only two years old. But in time we hope to have peaches, pears, and apples," said the older woman.

Soon we got to the residential hallway. The wall to our right was bare and on the left were doors spaced about every twenty feet. Exposed studs peeked out every now and then and the walls were a patchwork of oriented strand board and sheet rock. Each door was labeled with a number. 101-102-103-104. Once we got to 112, Olga stopped. "This is the first vacant one. There's not much inside," she said as she turned the knob and opened the door. "But we'll add more as time goes by, assuming you decide to stay."

"We'd like to see our friends," said Gus.

"They'll have taken Sam to the Real Estate office downstairs. It's where Doc set up shop," said the quirky woman. "

"Go ahead and make yourselves comfortable. We have a water tank rigged on the ceiling, so there's running water for showers It's just not heated beyond what the sun provides. I'll have someone set some fresh clothes in the hallway for you but you'll find soap and towels inside. There's bottled water in the kitchen and we'll feed you in a bit. Don't drink the water from the shower."

"Thanks," I said.

"Feel free to move about the building. Not many rules here, just common sense. We do ask that you mind rationing, don't fight, and always check weapons out if you need to use them."

"Got it," said Gus.

"I'll leave you to it, then."

"Thanks."

Olga turned and walked back down the hall. We watched until she turned the corner. Gus and I walked through the door into a dimly lit room. It was small but quaint, if not bare of furniture. Our footfalls echoed on the concrete floor. The exterior walls had exposed studs on our side. To our left was a small corner kitchen. It was the only corner that had sheet rock lining the inside. The walls that joined with the other units were much like the hallway walls; a patchwork of materials.

"We could make it homey," said Gus quietly. "Finish the walls. Paint. Maybe add a couch?"

"You're thinking of staying?" I asked.

My voice sounded empty of emotion.

"Maybe. I'm so tired of running, Zo."

"She's gone," I barely whispered.

Standing close to my side, Gus wrapped his arms around me and pulled me to him.

"She'll always be with us."

I buried my face into his chest and leaned on him.

"I feel like the biggest part of me has died with her." My voice was muffled against his chest.

"I have no words, darlin'. I wish I did. I think she took a huge part of both of us with her."

"I need to know what happened," I sighed heavily.

"We'll talk to their doctor. See if he has any insight. I'd like him to look at your arm, too."

I didn't answer, but rather closed my eyes and let him hold me. After a long moment he loosened his arms and looked down at me.

"Let's get cleaned up, then go check on Sam."

I nodded. "Yeah."

He used the pads of his thumbs to caress my face. His eyes held the deep sadness that I felt deep within my soul. I could also see worry and uncertainty reflecting back to me. He carefully helped me undress since my arm was still bandaged and hard to move.

"You've lost too much weight," he said in a sad tone.

"I'll be fine."

"We really should think about staying. Even if it's just for a little while. Let your arm heal. Regular meals. Time to catch our breath."

"Maybe."

By that point it was hard to trust anyone but my husband and Hoot. I had known them the longest of anyone left alive on earth.

"Let's go find the shower."

He took my uninjured elbow and gently led me to another corner of the large room. A rudimentary bathroom took up a corner of the only bedroom.

"It would have made a cute apartment, huh?" I asked, not really expecting an answer.

"I'm sure we can fix it up a bit."

"If we stay," I added.

"If we stay."

The shower in the bathroom hadn't yet been installed when the dead rose, but there was a drain pipe in the floor that had been rigged to a plastic kids wading pool. Plastic sheeting hung loosely from exposed studs, the ends falling into the kiddie pool. A hose dangled from the ceiling, the end capped with a shut-off valve. Nearby sat an old kitchen chair that was topped with several folded bath towels, hand towels, and washcloths. A bar of soap and bottle of shampoo were tucked under the chair.

We showered together, using the least amount of water we could.

CHAPTER 15

As promised, a pile of clean clothing waited for us in the hallway. Someone had guessed our sizes rather well. Everything was new, still with tags intact. Underwear from Target, sweat pants, leggings, and t-shirts from Walmart. The slippers left for Gus were a size too small, but manageable for inside use.

We dressed quickly. My arm was oozing after the shower and we had no bandages with which to dress it, so decided to find the medical area in search of Doc, Sam, and Hoot. Gus wrapped a hand towel loosely around my arm to avoid contamination and infection. As we walked to the door to the hallway, a knock sounded.

"Delivery," called out a male voice.

"Hold on," Gus called back while shrugging his shoulders at me.

"Hurry up, Gus!" called out the unmistakable voice of Hoot. "This mother's heavy!"

Gus rushed forward and opened the door inward. Hoot was on the back end of a mattress, the man in front unknown to us.

"Olga came down and said you'd need this in here. You're helping me carry one up for Sam later on. They're putting me and him next door, number 113."

"How is he?" I asked.

"Not great. Doc says he should live, but he needs to amputate."

"Oh my fucking God," said Gus with a tone of distress and a look of fear.

"He says it's infected, that gangrene has set in. He has him started on an IV drip with antibiotics and wants to operate in a couple hours."

"Fuck," said Gus as he ran his hand over his chin. "Poor Sam."

"Doc wants to see you both ASAP," said the stranger. "Name's Ed." He held his hand out and I shook it, followed by Gus.

"Just tell us where to go," I said.

I was beginning to feel the exhaustion that I knew would hit. I was anxious to see Sam and anxious to eat. My arm was also throbbing.

"We'll just carry this in then take you downstairs to them," said Ed.

"Chanel said she'd come back up and get a few things set up for you in here," said Hoot.

We stepped aside while the two men lifted the mattress across the threshold and carried it into what would become our bedroom.

"Let's go," said Ed.

Once we were in the hallway, Hoot draped an arm across my shoulders and pulled me close. He didn't say anything, but I knew his gesture was meant to comfort me. Meant to let me know he knew I was hurting deeply.

***

Doc's office was anything but traditional. He directed me to an exam room in the back corner of what had been a real estate office. The exam table was actually a professional folding massage table covered in a sheet that could easily be changed between patients. A single shelf held basics: rubbing alcohol, cotton balls, Band-Aids, cotton swabs, a jar of gauze pads. A blood pressure cuff was mounted to the wall with a stethoscope hanging beside it. A small wall-mounted cabinet with glass doors held several bottles of pills. It was padlocked shut.

Hoot waited in the larger room, where three twin beds were set up for sicker patients. Sam occupied one of them. I requested that Gus stay at my side.

"Your friend Hoot says you were shot," Doc said to me.

He looked like an old version of "Data" on Star Trek the Next Generation. And crazy. At the moment, though, he was very serious and I instantly felt like I was in good hands.

"Yeah. My arm."

"Mind if I take a look?"

"Not at all. Thanks."

I held my arm out and he unwrapped the towel.

"Hmm, looks pretty gruesome," he said, followed by an out of place chuckle. "Who patched it up?" he asked, looking between me and Gus.

"I did," said Gus.

"Did you get the bullet out?"

"Ayup. And stitched it."

"Looks like you did a fine job. You have medical experience?"

"Yes, sir. US ARMY Nurse Corps, four years."

"Good man. I imagine you got a lot of experience, well beyond most RNs."

"Ayup."

"Your friend Hoot said you gave her blood?"

I was beginning to feel a bit talked about while sitting there

"Yeah. She lost a lot. I'm O-negative, universal donor."

"Good thinking. You likely saved her life."

"Ayup. I think she needs antibiotics, though."

"Any allergies, young lady?" the doctor asked me.

"No. Well, just shrimp."

"We have some ampicillin on hand. Let's say two IV doses and then we can switch to pills."

"Sounds reasonable," said Gus.

"Hoot told us about Sam," I said as the doctor gently inspected my arm more closely.

"He's sleeping right now. He's on some pretty heavy pain killers. Unfortunately, there's nothing I can do to fix the break; we just don't have the resources or facilities."

"And you see signs of infection?" asked Gus.

144

"I do. He's also got a fever. I want this dose of antibiotics to go in before we prep him, but it needs to come off soon."

"Does he know?" I asked.

"Not yet," answered Doc.

"I should go wake him and tell him," Gus offered.

I looked up. "Let me?"

"Darlin', you don't have to do that. It won't be easy."

"I need to."

Gus sighed in clear disapproval.

"You've been through enough the past couple of days."

"Well," I said. "Time to go through one more fucked up thing."

"Hoot told me about your little girl. I'm really sorry to hear it," said the Doc.

I held back tears.

"You're both infected?" he asked for confirmation.

"Ayup."

"And the little one?"

"Hope," I said as clearly as I could without breaking down.

"Hope," repeated Doc.

"She had albinism. Rapid growth," Said Gus

"Hoot said she touched you, Zoe, and caused you to collapse."

I nodded.

"When Hope touched me, it burned us both," Gus added. "She died shortly after."

"Had this ever happened before? The burning?"

"No, never," I added quickly.

"I may know what happened. We've seen it once before. Not exactly the same, mind you, but I delivered a baby here. She seemed fine. I handed her to her mother. She was adjusting to life well, until her father picked her up. He had trouble catching his breath all of a sudden, to a point where Olga had to take the baby from his arms. He lived, but in the turmoil we hadn't noticed the infant struggling. Olga set her in a bassinet and the next time we checked on her, she had passed."

"Hope had been telling us not to touch her all of a sudden," I said.

"She knew," said Gus with a shaky voice. "She tried to warn us."

"It's possible the blood transfusion was a deadly combination," said the kooky old man.

"But she was part of both of us," I said, my voice barely a whisper "Why all of a sudden?"

"Once Gus' blood mixed with yours, it might have had an effect on her."

"But I held her. I slept with her after the transfusion."

"It's just a theory, but it may be like an allergy. Repeated exposure can eventually cause a reaction."

"So it was my fault," said Gus.

"Nothing like this is ever anyone's fault," Doc said. "If you want to blame anyone, blame the bastards who started this war."

Gus looked up. "Yeah if we only knew."

Doc looked surprised. "We're running off the terrorism theory. We had a guy come through here about a year ago. He was a journalist for CNN, taking a vacation in Seattle for his baby granddaughter's birth. He'd been hearing rumors through his contacts that radicals in the Middle East had developed a bio-weapon. Our paths crossed and he was with us for about a month. He didn't have hard facts, just rumors, but most of the puzzle pieces fit."

"Is there anywhere left? Anywhere safe" I asked.

"No one knows for sure. Society collapsed so fast. We have to assume the earth has been lost. We're just holding on the best we can. Hoping we can make it through somehow."

"It doesn't surprise me," said Gus. "If it is true. Things had been escalating in the Middle East for a while. They despised most of the modern world. At least the extremists did. They had the means and the will. *Son of a bitch*," he said, sounding pissed.

Doc sighed heavily.

"There'll be more time to talk about specifics later. My own lab findings. Compare notes. What we know as a group. What you all know. Olga should just about have our meager operating room ready and it's time to get Sam ready."

"Let me go talk to him," I said softly.

"Five minutes," said Doc.

I stood and walked past Hoot. Behind me, I could hear Gus and Doc talking about the treatment plan for my arm. As soon as I finished breaking the news to Sam, Olga would hook me up to an IV for antibiotics and bandage my arm. While she worked on me, Doc's assistants would help with Sam's amputation. I felt sick to my stomach as I sat down beside Sam. He looked puny in the small bed, but peaceful. I knew that was about to change.

His injured wrist was wrapped in blood-soaked gauze and sat on top of a disposable waterproof pad. An IV bag hung from the wall on his right, the tubing going into a vein near his elbow. I took hold of his right hand, careful to avoid his IV tube.

"Sam?" I called out to him, knowing my voice was too quiet to be effective.

"Sam," I said slightly louder as I squeezed his fingers.

His eyes flickered open, but his lids looked heavy.

"Zoe. I was waiting for you."

He tried to smile but it came out as a grimace.

"Sorry I took so long. I'm here with you though, okay?"

"Yes," he said slowly.

"Sam, I have to talk to you about your wrist."

"It's alright. I already know what they're going to do. You can't let them do it."

He began coughing.

"Their doctor says there's no choice. It's broken really bad, and infected."

"It's not that. I'm already dying. I'll be one of them soon. If they cut it off, then it'll be a detached hand alive forever and never be able to eat."

I placed my free hand on his forehead. He was so hot to the touch.

"It won't have a mouth. Or teeth."

"No, you're just delirious."

147

"O-kay," he said as he began to fall asleep again.

I kept my hand around his until Doc and a woman I hadn't met came to take him in to surgery. Gus and Hoot were not far behind them, rolling a stretcher.

"Margie, go ahead and give him 200 mics of fentanyl IV. Push it slow, over about three minutes. We'll transfer him to the gurney after it's hit."

"On it," the woman said.

Gus held a small IV bag and tubing in his hand, and what I recognized as an IV-start-kit in the other.

"Go ahead and give him some Phenergan too. Put it on a pump for 30 minutes."

"I'm not sure how to do that," she admitted, looking a bit embarrassed. "Olga hasn't shown me yet."

"It's okay, Margie. You can start the IV on Miss Zoe and hang her antibiotic. Just at a slow drip. Gus, can you help hang some Phenergan?"

"Sure. Is that okay with you, Zo?" he asked me.

"Whatever will help Sam the most. My own arm can wait."

"Just let me know where the supplies are," said Gus.

"You should find a pump and tubing in the closet to your left. The Phenergan is in the desk drawer by the back exit. Well, it's closed off, but it was the back exit."

Gus looked around until he saw the EXIT sign, which no longer glowed green. He left my side and my anxiety instantly rose.

"You ready?" Margie's soft voice was calming.

The girl was young; perhaps in her late teens at most.

"Sure."

"I'm Margie. Doc wants me to give you antibiotics so I need to start an IV."

"Sure," I said.

"Let's see, I can't do it on your injured arm so I'll try on the back of your other hand. I know it's an awkward place but I'm still new at this and it's the easiest. Usually."

"Do you have to do them a lot?" I asked, wondering how new she was at it.

"Not really."

"But you know how, right?" My anxiety was increasing rapidly.

"Oh," she paused. "Oh yeah…Doc's had me practice on him and his wife. And I started two last month on people that got hurt."

"How long do you think they'll take with Sam?"

I changed the subject to try to get my mind off the fact that I was likely just more practice for the girl.

"I'm not sure, to be honest."

Before I knew it, Margie finished inserting the IV cannula and taped it down to the back of my hand.

"Will he be asleep?" I asked.

"The drugs they gave him will help, but we don't have a way to do general anesthesia."

While I wanted to run away and cry, I forced myself to take a deep breath and keep my sadness and anger on the inside. Margie continued to prep the IV line for a dose of antibiotics and finished up by connecting it to the small line in my hand.

"He'll be okay. Doc's fast and he's done this once before."

"He told me to not let them do it."

"I think that's a normal response."

"I think he was delirious. He said he was dying and turning into one of them already."

"He has a high fever and is on strong pain meds. I'm sure he's just delirious. He'll need his friends to support him."

"Yeah. I know."

Minutes passed and my thoughts drifted to Hope, to Gus, to the people we had just lost in the old folk's home, and back to Sam in the next room. Margie sat beside me, watching the small IV bag to make sure it wasn't running in too fast, all while bandaging my arm.

"I'm sure you'll want to sleep after this," she said.

"Maybe. If I can."

"Doc can give you a sleeping pill. I can bring your next IV dose up when it's due. We'll keep Sam in here and one of us will be with him for at least the next twenty-four hours. As long as his fever breaks and his bleeding is controlled he can move upstairs after that."

As soon as she stopped talking, Sam's screaming jolted me to the core. It wasn't just a man screaming, it was the sound of torture and excruciating pain.

"Hold him down!" I heard someone yell. It must have been Doc.

"Sam, you have to hold still!" Gus.

Sam continued screaming. It was shrill and primal. My hand began to hurt where the IV was infusing. I looked down to realize my fists were clenched, as were my teeth. Margie sniffled and when I glanced at her she was physically shaking and her skin was two shades of pale. Slowly, Sam's screams began to subside. I wasn't sure how much time passed, but when I glanced at the IV bag it was empty. Margie looked up as well, and stood up to disconnect the IV line.

"We can do this part pretty fast and get you settled upstairs. I'll send your dad when he's done."

"My dad?"

"The Army nurse?"

I shook my head. "That's Gus, my husband."

The younger girl blushed, the new color in her cheeks standing out against the pastiness of her skin.

"Sorry," she mumbled.

"It's fine. Don't sweat it."

She seemed awkwardly uncomfortable and hurried with the last of her medication duties. Once she was satisfied, she unscrewed the longer line from the shorter one that would remain in my hand.

"I'll see you to the kitchen and then get you settled upstairs, then," she said.

"Thanks."

I didn't particularly want to go anywhere without Gus or Hoot, or Sam for that matter, but staying in that medical office knowing what had just happened was the worse option. As we left, I heard Sam sobbing.

***

150

Options in the kitchen were slim. Margie offered to cook an egg for me, but I declined. I was tired, so just grabbed an apple and a couple single-serve peanut butter packets. Before heading back upstairs, she explained that everyone is expected to eat during main meal times unless they're out scouting. In a situation like ours, where we had just arrived, picking a few items would be fine. She promised to walk Gus and Hoot through as well before sending them upstairs.

Leaving the kitchen, I realized it had grown late. Windows were all boarded except for every third, which had a small gap left at the top to allow for some light to enter.

"We're conserving batteries so try to only use them if you're up walking around. Keep them away from the windows. A candle in the kitchen is usually fine. We try to keep it dark at night 'cause the dead watch."

"They watch for any change," I echoed.

"Here we are. 112," she said awkwardly as we approached the door to my new unit. "You can take my flashlight. I know my way around well enough."

"Thanks," I said as I took the small flashlight from her.

"I'll be back in about seven hours for your next IV dose. I'll send a pain pill up with your husband."

"Just Tylenol. Save the stronger stuff for others."

"You sure?"

"Yeah."

"Okay. Good night then."

"Night."

I watched as she walked back down the hall. I opened the door and stepped inside. Slowly, I shined the flashlight around to get my bearings. The kitchen now held a small two-person patio table with mismatched folding chairs and a trash can. I walked through to the small living room, where a futon couch just big enough for two sat beneath the window. I could see into the bedroom through the open walls. A bed had been assembled. Not just the mattress, but a box spring and metal frame with simple wood head and foot boards. It was dressed in sheets and topped with a homey quilt. A nightstand sat beside the bed with a paper folded on top. I walked closer and picked it up. I used the flashlight to read a note.

Welcome home. There's water in the kitchen and a few basics. Meals are eaten downstairs by the kitchen, with breakfast at 8:30. Get a good night sleep and we'll go over basics before lunch.

-Chanel

Sitting on the edge of the bed, I turned off the flashlight and ate half the apple. Exhaustion took over. I left the other apple half and the peanut butter on the side table for Gus, stood, pulled the covers back, and climbed into the bed. The night was cold and my feet felt frozen, so I pulled the covers up to my chin and curled into a fetal position.

***

When I felt someone touch my wrist, my eyes flew open and I backed away, into Gus.

"It's okay. It's just Margie; I'm here to take out your IV."

"Margie," I said with a sigh of relief.

Gus scooted closer and wrapped an arm around me. I could tell by his breathing that he was still asleep.

"Don't I need another dose?" I asked.

"It's already done. You slept through it," she whispered.

"How's Sam?" I asked quickly.

"He's sleeping. Doc has him on a morphine drip and Hoot's sitting with him."

"Has Hoot slept? I can go trade him places," I said.

"No, you need to heal. We already have a volunteer coming to sit. Head down to the cafeteria for breakfast. I smell pancakes. They'll be serving for another half an hour."

"Thanks, Margie."

"No problem. I'll let Doc know you'll be in to visit Sam after breakfast. He'll want to change your bandage while you're there."

The tape being peeled off the back of my hand stung, but I was glad to be free of the IV catheter. I closed my eyes as she walked across our little apartment, and only vaguely heard the door open and shut. Our mattress was soft and the sheets comforting. It was a luxury to which I was no longer accustomed.

"Morning," mumbled Gus.

I rolled over to face him and he tightened his arm around me. "Hi."

"Did she say someone's makin' pancakes?"

"Yeah."

"Let's go eat. I'm starving."

"Okay," I said with a sigh.

"What's wrong?"

He reached under the blankets and found my hand, giving it a squeeze.

"Everything."

"I know. We still have to eat, though, darlin',"

"Tell me," I whispered. "Is Sam going to be okay?"

"I suspect so. I think Doc took care of him just in time. Once infection spreads to the blood, well, without advanced medicine he'd have been doomed. As it was Doc had to take a bit more than he'd expected."

"I feel so bad for him," I said as I nestled closer and buried my head against his bare chest.

Gus began to snore softly. I sighed.

"Gus," I said as I nudged at his shoulder.

"Hmm?"

"Pancakes."

As badly as I didn't want to feel hunger, or sadness, or anything, the thought of food was making me salivate.

"Ayup. On it."

"I need to pee," I said.

"Okay."

"I'm not sure where to go. There's no toilet in here."

"Number one or two?" he asked sleepily.

"One."

"Just squat in the shower, okay?"

"Ew."

***

It took us only minutes to get ourselves sorted before we left our apartment to make our way to the dining area. A few others were also heading to breakfast. No one looked familiar and a couple people took their time looking us over as we made our way down the hall and then the stairs.

"Do you remember where to go?" I asked.

"Once we get to the main floor it's on the left."

We made our way down the last set of steps and found the dining room quickly. There were a handful of people sitting at round tables, all seemingly enjoying their meals. Chanel saw us and waved us over.

"Grab your plates by the window and help yourselves. It's usually buffet style. You'll see a little chalk board to the right of the food that says what the limit is per person. Leftovers are fair game once everyone's done. What's not eaten is fed to the compost pile in the courtyard."

"Thanks," Gus said for both of us.

"Doc knows you'll be heading over to check on Sam and he wants to look at your arm, Zoe," she said.

"Thank you," I said.

The woman gave me a quick and gentle hug.

Gus took my hand and pulled me away to the food counter. I could feel curious eyes upon us. Paper plates were in a neat stack, with plastic flatware in a basket. We each took a plate and peeked at the chalkboard.

Pancakes 2
Eggs 1 scoop
Bell peppers 3 slices
Syrup 2 packets

We loaded our plates with our share and found two empty seats in the back. The pancakes were small and the eggs cold. As far as we were concerned, though, it was a feast. While my mood remained somber, the food hitting my stomach felt good. Halfway through the meal, Hoot sat down across from me.

"Hey, Hoot," said Gus with his mouth full.

"Hey."

"Jesus, brother. You look like shit."

"It was a rough night. Sam's not looking so hot."

His attention grabbed, Gus swallowed and sat up straighter. "How so?"

"He's lost a lot of blood. He's pale. He's still burning up. Saying all kinds of weird shit."

"Who's with him now?" I asked.

"Doc's wife, Olga. She just gave Sam some IV morphine so he was asleep when I left."

"You need to catch a few winks too," said Gus.

"I plan to. I guess they set me up in the unit next to you two. Sam and I will be bunking together once he can leave the infirmary."

Wanting to see Sam as soon as possible, I began to eat faster. My stomach filled half a pancake shy of clearing my plate, so I scooted it toward Hoot.

"Finish it?" I pleaded.

He nodded. "Thanks, Zoe. You guys go ahead and stop in to see Sam. I'll clear your plates."

We both stood and Gus patted Hoot on the back. I leaned down and kissed him on his scruffy cheek.

"Go sleep," I whispered.

"Yes, ma'am."

***

Gus and I left the cafeteria. I followed him to the infirmary, this time taking notice of which turns led where. The medical room seemed smaller than it had the night before.

"Gus. Zoe," said Olga, who looked exhausted. "Doc's in with Sam now."

"Olga? What's wrong?" I asked.

Her face was drawn and read like a very sad story.

"He's not doing too well. Fever hasn't broken and Doc thinks the infection's spread."

155

"Fuck," mumbled Gus under his breath.

"Can I see him?" I asked.

"Of course. He's not very lucid, though, just to warn you."

She led us to the back corner, where a partition was in place for Sam's privacy.

"Doc, Sam's friends are here."

"Send 'em right in, my little bird."

Doc's voice sounded haggard, and when we stepped to the other side of the divider screen his face agreed. Sam lay on the bed face up, sweat coating his face in a waxy mask. His color was a hue of gray. I knew at first glance that his chances were slim. His chest rose and fell irregularly. His eyes were closed. His stump lay next to him, blood seeping through the bandage and onto the sheets.

"It's not looking good," the doctor said. "Whatever this infection is, it's spreading fast and I can't seem to catch up to it."

"Is he still just on ampicillin?" asked Gus.

"It's all we have, but I doubled the dose."

"We'll head out and find something else," I said curtly.

"No, darlin'. There's no time."

I felt like I had no energy left. None for anger, or sadness, or to question either of the men.

"Then let me sit with him. As long as it takes."

Doc sighed. "I can't deny you that."

"What's that smell?" I asked.

"The infection," said Doc.

I nodded and walked to Sam's bedside. A wingback chair had been brought in, and I sat gingerly. I reached out and took Sam's remaining hand in mine. He took a shuddering breath and moved his head side to side.

"There's no use," he mumbled.

"Sam?" I called to him.

"There's no point, Whitney. Everyone is gonna die."

I wasn't sure who Whitney was.

"Shhh, rest," I tried to soothe him.

His eyelids fluttered but he didn't wake up. His hair was soaking wet and plastered to his forehead. His hand in mine felt so hot.

"It's okay to let go," I said softly. "It'll be okay, friend."

While I hadn't known him for very long, Sam was like family. I didn't want him to die, but I also didn't want him to suffer.

He cried out and grimaced.

"It hurts," he moaned. A tear fell from his eye and ran down his temple and onto the bed.

"Doc?" I called.

"I heard. I'm bringing morphine now."

"She's gone, Zoe. Hope's dead."

I used my other hand to caress his forehead.

"I know. We lost her on the bus."

"They have her now," he said as he began sobbing again.

"Who has her, Sam?"

"The smoke monsters. They're so dark and she's so bright it hurts to look at her."

His words caused a shiver to run up my spine. Doc and Gus moved the curtain aside and stepped to the other side of the bed. Doc reached across the bed to access the IV port, which was in the arm I was holding onto. He screwed a syringe onto the line and slowly pushed clear liquid. Within seconds, Sam relaxed and was once again asleep.

"He's delirious," said Gus. "You can't try to read into what he said about Hope."

"I know." It was all I could say.

I don't think he'll be with us long, darlin'. You don't have to stay and watch."

"Yes, I do. We owe him that much."

"I'll stay with you," he offered.

"No. Let me do this alone. You can be there for me afterward."

He sighed heavily but knew me well enough to know to not argue. I hadn't been able to be there for Hope, or Emilie, or Boggs…the list went on…but I would be there for Sam.

In the background, I heard Gus and Olga and Doc talking to each other. I took hold of Sam's hand again and leaned against the bed in which he fitfully rested. The skin of his hand had grown cold and clammy; only moments before it had been so hot. His chest rose and fell unevenly. Every now and then he'd cry out incoherently. It was hard to tell if it was a sound of pain or fear or from some other reason. When Doc and Gus came back, I didn't move from my position or look away from Sam. They each took position on either side of the bed and began tying our friend to the frame of the bed.

"Do you have to?" I asked.

"You know we do, darlin'. You know what'll happen after he's gone."

"I know. I can take care of him before he turns," I said quietly.

I smoothed his hair back from his forehead, which was still hot.

"No," said Gus firmly.

"No?" I asked, irritated.

"Sorry, darlin', but I won't budge on this. If you're alone with him, this is how it'll be."

"Fine," I forced the word out.

They continued to apply the restraints. His amputated arm presented the biggest problem, so was left unbound. A soft strap was used to hold his chest down. Neither of the men said anything before stepping out, but Gus rested a hand on my shoulder and squeezed gently.

Sam and I were left in relative silence. I kept his hand in mine and lay my head on the edge of the bed. I knew he was gone when his hand clenched mine briefly and then went slack.

"Oh Sam," I whispered. "I'm so sorry I couldn't fix this."

I had no tears to offer; they had run dry. Instead, I folded his one hand over his belly and stood. I leaned down and kissed his forehead. His eyelids were partly open and his eyes already looked clouded. It's amazing how quickly a person transforms from the living into the dead. Within seconds their life force is visibly gone. It's the subtle things: lack of the rise and fall of the chest, skin no longer moving over pulse points, even cheeks become concave in the blink of an eye. Sam was there, and in a matter of seconds he was just – gone.

I sat back down and took his cold, still hand in mine once again. I leaned against the side of his bed and rested my head on my arm. Focusing on when we first met Sam became a mental goal, and so I closed my eyes and focused. It seemed like years ago, not just days. Why I felt such a strong connection to him I wasn't sure. Perhaps because I had worked so hard to save him during the tornado. Perhaps we were kindred spirits. There'd would be no chance to find out.

Still unable to feel Gus within myself, the only clue that he was behind me was his breathing.

"It's time, darlin'."

"I want to stay until he's really gone," I mumbled against my arm.

He set a hand on my shoulder. When I didn't respond, he wrapped his arms around me in a loving embrace from behind.

"It's all been too much. He's gone and it's time to say good-bye."

"I can't, Gus. I can't lose anyone else."

Just before he began emitting a pathetic moan, Sam's hand gripped mine. It was a cold, stiff grip marked with small twitches. I tensed, knowing he had woken up. Gus kept a firm yet gentle grip on me.

"Doc," called Gus. "It's time."

"We're here," said the older man. "Olga, help hold his arm down, doll?"

"Zoe, Doc's going to take a blood sample before we leave."

I nodded, knowing there was a reason, likely research.

Sam's body quickly became active and fought the restraints.

"Hold him still," said Doc curtly.

"I need to help," Gus whispered as he kissed my cheek.

He let go of me and I stood.

"Tell me what I can do," I said, exhausted but knowing they could use help.

"Be a dear and hold his legs down at the knee caps," said Olga. "Gus if you can get his other arm and neck that'd be peachy," she continued.

I thought to myself that 'peachy' was an odd word to use under the circumstances. I refrained from laughing, mostly out of fear of being labeled insane. Holding Sam's knees down proved difficult. I simply wasn't tall enough. Doc fought to obtain a sample of blood and the task seemed to grow more difficult with each breath I took. One of Sam's feet sideswiped me face, knocking me off balance momentarily.

"Hold up," I said. "I need to get a better grip."

"Climb onto the bed," said Olga in an even voice.

I was in the process of doing just that when she suggested it. Doc took a step back as Olga released the dead man's stump in order to still one of his legs while I got situated. Sam's jaws snapped toward Gus hungrily. As I knelt on one leg to still it, a quick glance at Sam's face left me with no doubt whatsoever that he was in no way the man we had known. I placed both of my hands on either side of his knee while my body weight held down the other leg. Olga's arm muscles strained against the force of his stump working against her. The dead man nearly got ahold of Doc's upper arm as he bent over for another attempt to draw blood.

"Keep him steady," the doctor said smoothly. "I'm almost done."

"Zo, babe, stay on his legs till Olga and I get there to take over."

All of a sudden the corpse below grew still.

"No need," said Doc.

I looked up to see him still holding a knife that was embedded into Sam's ear.

I sighed party from exhaustion and partly from sadness, but was glad it was over, for Sam's sake.

CHAPTER 16

Days passed, one blending into the next. The sadness of losing Hope continued to fill my heart and occupied my mind without respite. Gus would scream her name in his sleep almost nightly. The two of us had grown distant since her death. I suppose we were a reminder to each other of the good and beauty we had brought into the world and then lost. My arm healed but ached by bedtime each day. I spent most of my days in the gardens pulling weeds and helping harvest as crops matured. Gus spent most of his time on top of the cargo containers on border patrol. I got into the habit of taking my meals to our little apartment, not wanting to face other people. The group as a whole disapproved, saying social isolation was dangerous. Once bedtime hit, Gus would come home late and I'd already be in bed.

Time had little meaning in our new lives at the compound. Days of the week blended together. It was either dark or light, and I didn't bother to track the actual time. Ash from the eruption of Mt. Rainier wasn't thick where we had settled, but enough had accumulated in small drifts here and there that the scouting parties would bring back sacks full on occasion to put into the garden for fertilization. The idea had been mine, and I hated the praise I was given. I wanted to be invisible.

***

The heat of summer hit in full force. This close to the Scablands of Washington felt like Hell on earth. Nights were seldom much cooler than daytime, and sleeping in our room grew uncomfortable. Most of my time was spent in solitude as

162

Gus began doing patrol overnight. A crew was actively digging into the earth just outside the border, with the intention of lowering some of the cargo containers into the earth to be partially buried. They would double as safe rooms in the event of a horde as well as cooler sleeping quarters during the heat.

Plants watered and weeds pulled, I was done for the morning when Chanel approached me.

"A few of us are headed outside the walls on a scavenging run. Hoping you'll come with us?" she asked.

"Oh, I don't know. There's a lot to do here," I said.

"We'll only be gone a few hours. You need to get out, Zoe."

I sighed, knowing she was right.

"Where are you going?" I asked.

"Just a supply run. We're taking a bad-ass truck so we can haul a lot. It's just us girls this trip. There's a town nearby called Winthrop so we'll start there. We've already cleared most of the stores but there's a small nursery a few miles outside of town we'll hit up."

"Well…okay," I said a bit hesitantly.

I really didn't want to go, but gave in. Maybe the change in routine would do me good.

"I'm just about to take some water to the construction crew. We'll be leaving in ten. I'll let Gus know you're headed out with us."

"No."

"No?" she asked, quizzically.

"No. He'll just worry. Let him focus on his work."

"You sure?"

"Yeah." I paused briefly. "Positive."

The truth was I knew he'd protest my leaving the security of the compound.

"Okay. Go ahead and check out your weapons of choice from Arnie and meet us down in the parking garage in a few minutes."

She walked away and I wrapped my arms around myself, suddenly feeling a slight thrill at the thought of going on the run. I hurried to the weapon's room, where I picked out a hunting knife and a revolver with extra ammo.

Arriving at the parking garage, I was met by two women that weren't much older than Chanel and myself. I had seen them in the kitchen and laundry areas a few times but had never said much more than "hi" to them. The taller of the two, Kendall, nudged the shorter as I approached.

"Hey Zoe," said the shorter of the two. "Chanel said you're coming with today. Glad to have you on board."

"You know my sister Brenda, right?" asked Kendall.

I smiled half-heartedly. "I don't think we've really formally met," I said.

"You work in the gardens most of the time, right?" asked Brenda.

"Yeah. It feels kinda peaceful."

"That's hard to come by nowadays…a sense of peace."

"Yeah."

An awkward silence fell between us, broken only by one of the sisters suggesting we go ahead and climb into the truck.

"You can sit up front with Chanel if you want," said one of them.

"I heard my name?" asked Chanel as she walked toward us.

"Yeah. I'm up front with you," I said.

"Good. We can chat about some plans I have, if you don't mind?"

"Sure."

We all took seats in the truck. A crew cab, it was more than large enough for the four of us and the scant gear that Brenda and the sisters pre-packed.

"What's up with the backpacks?" I asked, eyeing four of them in the middle of the back seat.

"Bug-out bags. In case we get stuck anywhere," explained Kendall.

"Wear it when we're out of the truck. There's some basics: water, dried food, a flashlight, some basic tools. Enough to last a day or two as long as you ration," continued Brenda.

"Awesome," I said in a flat tone.

"Relax," urged Chanel. "It's just in case."

"Okay. Let's get going. I want to get back before dark," said Kendall.

Chanel turned the key and the pick-up revved to life. None of us bothered with seat belts. Hitched to the back of the pickup was an open trailer with decent-height wooden side rails. Chanel handled the set-up well. Olga and a man named Drew opened the gate for us, and we were on our way.

***

The landscape had changed since we had first arrived at our new home. Trees were full of green leaves and dotted the hillsides in seas of green.

"They're mostly peach and apple," said Chanel. "Orchards as far as you can see. We'll come back when it's time to harvest."

"Do you think there's anyone left out there?" I asked, rather randomly.

"We have to hope so."

The road was bumpy from lack of maintenance, and deserted vehicles dotted the shoulders.

"We've cleared the highway for miles," said Brenda over the noise of the wind rushing in through open windows. "Depending on how far we go, we may need to shove a few more off to the shoulder."

"What kinds of things should I be looking for, once we get there?" I asked.

The excitement of the trip was starting to set in.

"Really anything useful. Medicine, food, seeds, tools. Clothes. You name it."

"I saw a bunch of fancy white geese last time I was out," said Kendall. "If they're still there I'd like to try to catch some."

Chanel snorted as she laughed. "Good luck with that!"

"No, really," continued Kendall. "I've thought about it a lot. If we can herd them into a building or something, we could catch a few. Think about, another source of eggs. Goose and dumplings. Fertilizer."

"We'll see," said Chanel with a sigh.

We drove along in silence, aside from the wind, for several minutes. I mulled over the goose idea.

"She's right," I said suddenly.

"Huh?" Brenda asked.

"The geese. We could use them," I continued.

Chanel chuckled.

"We'll need to look for some sort of cages, then stop for the geese on the way home," said Brenda.

"Sure," said Chanel with an alarming change to her tone.

"What is it?" I asked.

"Dead ahead. I don't like the look of it."

"Where?" Kendall asked from the back seat.

"The dark blue pickup on the left. Do either of you remember seeing it there before?"

The girls in the back both got quiet for a moment.

"I don't remember," said Brenda. "Maybe?"

"I don't," said Chanel.

"Slow down just a bit," I suggested.

Chanel took her foot off the gas but didn't apply the brake.

"See how clean it looks? It hasn't been there for long. At least not as long as the other vehicles," I added.

"I'm going to pull off at least fifty yards before we get there. Get your guns ready, and when I pull over get out through the passenger side and stay down, and grab your bug out bags too," said Chanel, who seemed to naturally take charge.

As the truck slowed to a stop, I took my pistol out, made sure the cartridge was full, and chambered a round. Swinging my pack onto one shoulder, I opened the door as soon as we were no longer in motion. I hopped down to the ground and rolled to the side to make room for Chanel. Kendall landed right after I did and our eyes met. It seemed an eternity before the other two joined us.

"What next?" Brenda asked in a whisper.

"We need to figure out if there's someone with the truck," said Chanel more calmly than I felt.

"Want me to go look?" asked Kendall.

"No. I want you on the back corner of the truck. Watch for any movement and be ready to shoot. Bren, same thing with you but at the front corner," instructed Chanel.

"What about me?" I asked.

"Think your arm can handle sliding under the truck with me?" she asked in reply as she glanced at the gnarled scar on my forearm. She was one of the only people I confided to about the ongoing pain.

"Yeah."

"Stay to my left. We're just going to go under and watch for any movement."

I removed my bug-out bag from my shoulder and wiped my hands on my jeans. Alongside Chanel, I slithered under the truck. It was a lifted body but there still wasn't much room to spare. The heat from the sun grew intolerable. The front driver's side tire provided some protection as we surveilled the truck. The asphalt rippled with little thermal waves, constantly tricking my eyes and causing me to think I saw actual movement on the other side of the highway.

"See the back of the truck?" I asked.

"What am I looking for?" she asked.

"It's hard to see with the ripples. Look at the ground just behind the back tire. It looks dark."

"Maybe just a shadow."

"No. Look at the other shadows near it. It's darker than the rest."

"Any ideas?" she asked.

"Not really. Could be oil. Or blood."

"I'm not seeing any movement. One of us needs to go over and check it out. The truck. The dark spot. All of it."

"I'll go," I said quickly.

"Let's back out and talk to Bren and Kendall."

We retreated from our perch under the truck and waved the others nearer. A crow flew overhead, cawing at something only it could see. Aside from that single bird, silence surrounded us. The four of us looked at each other before Chanel spoke.

"We didn't see any movement, just a dark spot on the road at the back of the truck. Zoe's volunteered to go look but the whole thing makes me nervous. If they're survivors we need to offer help, but if they have ill intentions, we don't want to lead them home."

"Or it could be a trap," said Kendall.

"Or that," agreed Chanel.

"Or that," I echoed flatly as I suddenly stood.

Chanel reached for me, but I was faster. As I walked to the front of our own truck, I mumbled about how there was only one way to find out. I held my breath as my head cleared the top of the hood, leaving me exposed to gunfire. Shots didn't come and I made my way to the street, weapon at the ready. A light breeze blew, stirring a few stray hairs that escaped my braid.

"Zoe! Come back!"

Already nearly to the other truck, I held up a hand. I saw nothing at all that was suspicious, aside from the truck and what indeed looked like a pool of blood at the tailgate. I kept my pistol aimed ahead as I got within arm's reach of the vehicle. Inside the cab was a disaster. Magazines, Twinkie wrappers, cigarette butts, and empty beer cans were strewn about. After I made sure no one was inside the cab, I quickly flattened my back to the driver's door and look to each side of me. Still nothing notable to see, I turned back around and quickly walked to the back of the pickup. I could tell by the smell of iron the puddle was indeed blood. The top layer was already forming a layer of glumpy clots, indicating it hadn't been spilled long ago but was also not completely fresh. I finished clearing the perimeter, all while constantly scanning the nearby shadows for any signs of danger. The situation was odd and gave me the willies. I held up a hand to signal the other women to stay on the other side of the road. I saw no reason for them to reveal their presence, just in case we were being watched.

I proceeded to climb into the back of the truck. The top edge of the tailgate was slick with gore, causing my stomach to drop a bit. I wiped my soiled palms on my jeans and proceeded forward, toward an ice chest. It was large, taking up more than half the width of the truck bed. Blood was smeared around the edges of the container with one unmistakable handprint centered on the white lid. My heart pounded as I considered opening it. I squatted in front of it, ready to spring up and run if needed. Preparing for the worst, I used my hands to leverage the lid open. The sight inside was not what I had expected to find. I became so overwhelmed by the loss of life that I didn't notice someone behind me.

"What is it?" asked Chanel gently as she placed a hand on my shoulder.

I found myself not able to answer.

"Aww, shit," said Chanel, echoing my feelings.

I forced myself to take a couple of deep breaths. "I hope it was quick," I said in a small shaky voice. "They couldn't have been more than a couple days old."

I used the back of my hand to wipe away a tear that threatened to fall. The twin babies were naked, attached at the pelvis. A third deformed leg twisted around to their front. It only had a rudimentary stub for a foot. The umbilical cord the babies had shared was larger than normal, the base taking up a large portion of their shared abdomen. It hung precariously to one side, dangling precariously as if might tear away from the babies at any moment. The cord itself was tied into a knot and still several inches long. The baby on the left seemed to be eternally staring at his brother. While layers of moist skin peeled from them, it was still clear that they had lighter streaks littering their bodies.

"I'm sorry, Zoe. I know it's really tough for you."

"Yeah," I responded.

"Let's get going. There's nothing left here. Brenda and Kendall are waiting in the truck."

"I wonder who the blood is from," I said as I tried to collect myself.

"Impossible to say. C'mon. Let's get out of here."

I closed the lid on the cooler, sealing the babies back inside. Chanel and I climbed out of the pickup bed and made our way back to our own vehicle.

The sisters had climbed back into the truck, Brenda behind the wheel with Kendall beside her. Chanel and I climbed into the back seats.

***

Once we entered the town of Winthrop, I was surprised to see so many of the buildings were intact. It was a small town. Tall pine trees bordered the main street, making it rather picturesque. On one side of the street, the storefronts were all connected by an old fashioned wood plank walkway. Each store blended into the next: *Wall's Ice Cream Parlor, Carlos' Barber Shop, The Teatime Café, Wendall's Books, Olde Towne Apothecary*...

"We got tons of meds from the town pharmacy over a year ago, but it's empty now. There were no signs of break-ins, so we're guessing there's some locals left here."

"Where?" I asked.

"Your guess is as good as anyone's," said Kendall. "Probably in hiding somewhere."

"We need to take a detour through the east part of town. The main highway has a semi truck overturned in the middle of it, blocking access. We've never bothered moving it since there's an alternate road. It just ads a few minutes," said Chanel.

"I want to be in and out within about ten minutes or so," said Brenda.

"Bren's our resident planner for this kinda stuff. She comes up with some wild predictions and statistics on risks."

"Cool," I said, for lack of anything else to say.

"Focus on finding anything that might help us back home. Fertilizer. Seeds. Rain barrels. Tools. You guys know the routine," added Brenda.

"What routine?" I asked.

"Sorry, I think Bren forgot you're new to our routine. She waits with the truck. Any signs of danger she'll whistle first and

170

shoot second. You hear either, then hightail it back to the truck," said Kendall with a yawn.

I got the impression she was tired of the routine.

"Got it," I said.

"Take your backpack with you. Always," warned Brenda. "You never know when you might not get back to the truck in time."

I smiled at her. "Point well taken."

We continued driving, winding through the now-empty streets until the town was behind us. Once back on the main highway, with the overturned semi impressively close to blocking the on-ramp, we picked up speed. There were fewer abandoned cars on that stretch of road. An old barn sat in a dilapidated heap off to the right, the earth threatening to reclaim it at any time.

"That's the old Cotter homestead," informed Chanel. "They were early settlers around here. Somewhere in that field there's the ruins of a fireplace from their first cabin."

"It looks like it's about to disappear," I said.

"Yeah. One day it'll be gone. One day all of this will," she said with a heavy sigh.

"Corpse at 2 o'clock," said Kendall.

"Should we stop and kill it?" I asked.

"Nah. Not with just one," said Brenda.

The Roamer in the field looked pathetically decayed. Its clothes were hanging in tatters, but oddly in better shape than the creature's decomposing skin. It swung its body as our truck passed, as if wanting to hitch a ride.

"Nasty bastards," mumbled Chanel.

"I'm surprised we haven't seen more," I said.

"Hey, is it true you used to be able to sense when they're around?" asked Kendall.

She turned to look at me.

"Yeah. Gus thinks I was infected the day this all started. For some reason it left me with the curse of them filling my head. I haven't been able to sense them, though, since just before we ended up with all of you."

"Was it pretty cool?" pressed Kendall.

I looked at her, my eyes wide. "No. It sucked. I could feel their hunger. See through their eyes. It was miserable."

"I hadn't thought of that," she admitted.

"Okay kids, time to go. The nursery's just around this bend on our left. Remember, quick-in, quick-out."

Within moments, the nursery came into view. It wasn't much to look at: a chain link fence that was leaning badly along one side, two greenhouse tent frames that wore ragged plastic covers, and a building about the size of a high school gymnasium.

Brenda pulled into the parking lot, swerving to avoid a large pothole, and carefully backed the truck up in front of the main entrance.

"Okay, let's go. I'll open the front door and make some noise. Zoe, Kendall, be ready in case there's any dead shitheads that creep up?"

I opened the crew cab door, slid down to the ground, swung my backpack over both shoulders, and readied my pistol.

"Let's go," I said.

Brenda stayed behind with the truck while the rest of us made our way to the main door of the nursery. Someone at some point had spray painted a large orange X across the swinging doors. The paint had faded and much was worn away, but the letters *c-l-e-a-r* were still legible.

"Looks like someone got here before us," said Kendall.

"Look," I said to get their attention. "There's a note."

On the left side of the door was a weathered plastic sleeve with a folded piece of paper inside. Something was scribbled in cursive. Chanel reached inside and removed the paper.

"It looks pretty damaged," she said.

As she unfolded it, spots of black mold and faded ink blended together. Very few words were legible.

Headed…a's..Prairie. Safe inside…we lost…stay…

"What do you think it says?" asked Kendall.

"Impossible to say," I said.

"Let's get inside so we can hurry and get back home," said Chanel.

"Should we break the glass?" asked Kendall.

"I have a better idea," I said as I approached the plastic sleeve that held the note.

Reaching inside, I pulled out a rusting key. The front doors were held shut by a metal chain and padlock. The key and lock were both weathered and rusted, causing the key to resist entry. Eventually it wiggled in, and the lock tumblers moved when I turned the key.

"Nice," said Kendall.

"I didn't even see the damned key in there," said Chanel.

I unwrapped the metal chain, taking care to make the least amount of noise possible. Once the door handles were free, I looked at the other two women, who both nodded at me. I placed one hand on the door handle and tightened my grip on my pistol with the other. Holding my breath, I pushed the door inward. I was met with silence. I slowly exhaled and worked my way into the dimly lit store. I resisted the urge to cough when dust invaded my lungs. I looked back at Kendall and Chanel briefly. They, too, were on high alert. The tension on their faces was easy to read.

A four-sided wire display rack lay on the floor by my feet. It appeared to have been knocked over in a hurry as seed packets littered the floor. I kept my pistol aimed in front of me and walked toward a pair of metal shelves that at one time held store stock. Now, they were empty.

"I'll check the back," said Kendall.

"Zoe, can you grab the seeds off the floor? It's better than leaving with nothing."

"Yeah, sure."

"I'm gonna search the registers. If we're lucky something got left behind."

"'Kay."

I knelt down and began picking up packets of seeds. More than half of them were damp, rendering them useless. It didn't take long to pick and choose. Sunflowers, cucumbers, red leaf lettuce, pumpkin, kale, cauliflower, onions, and corn were amongst those salvageable. As I began to stand the air in the large room grew heavy and uncomfortable. I tightened my grip on my gun and focused on all of my senses. For the first time in months, the one sense I had been cursed with alarmed inside of my mind. It was no more than the faintest of a tickle, but unmistakable. I quickly turned around in a circle, searching for the source. Seeing nothing, I backed up toward the cash registers, where I hoped to cross paths with Chanel.

Without knowing where either of the other two women were, exactly, I kept my pistol aimed slightly toward the floor for safety. Whatever was invading my mind felt far away, but was quickly approaching our location.

"Chanel," I called quietly.

"Over here," she called back, not taking much care to keep quiet.

"Shhh!" I snapped.

Hearing the strain in my voice, she too took a stance of caution.

"What is it?" she asked.

"There's dead near. Where's Kendall?"

"How do you know?"

"Don't ask. Not now. We need to get Kendall and go," I said with urgency.

"She took some bags of potting soil out to the pickup," she whispered back.

"Let's go. *Now*."

I picked up my bug-out bag and swung it over my shoulder as we made our way to the front door. Chanel reached for the handle, but I pulled her arm back.

"Don't," I cautioned.

"We have to warn them."

"It's too late. Look just to the right of the door," I said.

"Oh God, no…" moaned Chanel.

Just to the right of the building store front, a leg rested in a pool of blood. I recognized Brenda's boot, down to the hot pink laces. Severed at the thigh, strands of bloody flesh clung to the concrete. It was surreal seeing it not attached to a body.

"Maybe Kendall's okay," I said to try to calm Chanel. My voice was strained and clearly full of horror, only making matters worse.

Her face was pained and her eyes red. I knew she was full of initial grief, but also deep anger.

"We won't be any good to her if we're dead too," I continued. "Let's be smart and keep alert. Let's try for the roof, where we can see what's going on?" I suggested.

Chanel nodded.

"There's a mezzanine above the registers. I think we can get out one of the windows up there," she whispered.

A violent growl sounded outside, causing the glass doors to rattle.

"Fuck me," grumbled Chanel through a clenched jaw.

I pulled on her sleeve as I made my way toward the cash registers. Along the side wall, hidden in shadow, was a narrow wooden staircase. We hurriedly climbed as the monstrous sounds outside intensified.

The mezzanine was small, dark, and dusty. Boxes were stacked neatly at one end and a cot and blanket at the other. A single window overlooked the side yard of the building. Cries of agony rang out somewhere below and not too far away. It was impossible to say if it was Brenda, but I had a hard time imaging she might still be alive. There was too much blood from her amputation. Chanel and I looked at each other in understanding. I motioned upward. The building didn't feel safe. The doors were unlocked and whatever was outside had easy access to us where we stood. The roof was our best bet. With luck, we'd be able to go out the window and climb up.

"Now," I whispered.

We knelt below the small window. Chanel disengaged the small slide bolt and I removed a poor man's lock - a length of thick wood dowel - that kept it from opening upward.

The air around us grew still and heavy. Glass shattered below, immediately followed by a wet grunting noise. The smell of decay followed.

"Go," I whispered urgently.

The stillness of the air was relieved only by the fresh air streaming in from the newly open window. Chanel climbed through the opening head-first, twisting her body as she pulled her butt through.

"Zoe, there's just a sketchy metal ladder. I'm not sure it'll hold both of us, or even one of us."

The growling and grunting closer, a shiver ran up my spine. As soon as her knees cleared the sill, I began my own exit. Just like old times, my hip was throbbing and my mind was filled with sensations that did not belong to me. The incessant hunger of the dead was absent, and in its place anger and hate ran deep. I was certain I could feel one above other. I wasn't aware of what it wanted at that moment, but my instinct to put distance between it and myself was urgent.

"Go," I growled, urging Chanel to climb faster.

The roof was at least twenty feet above her, and the ladder ended just shy of the edge. Undaunted by the lack of a rung to reach the flat roof, Chanel grabbed onto the edging and hoisted herself upward. The intensity of the creature inside the building was audible to us both, but its inner desires were my burden to bear. I was nearly to the top of the ladder when Chanel toppled to safety. As I reached to grab the last rung, the building shook. I lost my footing, leaving me dangling by my injured arm. Searing pain traveled from my shoulder to my fingertips. The creature below was aware that we were no longer inside, driving it mad with anger. Dangling precariously, I looked up to the roof. Chanel leaned over the edge and reached down to me. I found a rung of the ladder with my feet to steady myself. The ceaseless growling of the creature grew irritatingly loud from the open window below. I hoisted myself upward as fast as I could, eventually landing on my side on the rooftop.

I surveyed the surface quickly. The flat roof was barren of ash, but served as home to years of fallen leaves and debris and was littered with puddles of stagnant rain water. In a far corner a small metal structure with a large fan built into one side beckoned to us. I drew my gun, as did Chanel, and we ran for the structure. The building shook again, this time feeling like a deep rumble. The screams of the creature below changed to sounds of a brawl; the grunts and moans and cries of more than one creature. My head was filled with rage, but now also fear.

"Whatever's in there, we need to split before their attention is back on us," I said quickly.

"What do you mean?"

"They're fighting. I don't know why. We need to get to the truck."

I got on my belly and scooted to the edge of the roof, which extended vertically and provided about two feet of cover. I had already lost my bearings and was unsure if we were at the front edge of the store or not. I got into a crouching position and looked over the edge. Sluggish Roamers surrounded us, but were still a good hundred feet away. The truck was thankfully below, Brenda's leg nearby. A wide streak of blood led away from the truck.

"There's a dumpster just below us," I said hurriedly.

Without thinking about the distance, I swung my leg over the edge and prepared to jump.

"Zoe, no! We can't leave Kendall."

"We have no idea where she is. If we don't go, whichever one of those monsters below us that wins is going to kill us both."

Chanel looked at me with horror in her eyes.

"The best thing we can do is get to safety. We can go back home and get help. If she's still alive…"

"Stop!" snapped Chanel.

"If she's still alive," I continued, "we may be her only hope of help. She has her bug-out bag. Give her some credit."

I was growing irritable over her hesitation. The Roamers were slow, but still getting closer. The beasts below us were thankfully still occupied with each other. Getting to the truck and getting out of there was our best chance, and perhaps our only chance.

I turned away from her and swung my other leg over. Looking back one last time, I whispered.

"It's now or never."

With those words, I wrapped my arms around my torso and let myself fall over the edge.

CHAPTER 17

Falling onto sacks of old trash hurt more than I could have imagined.

The pain of another human landing on top of me was just as bad, if not worse. As Chanel landed on my right side, the force pushed my head against the edge of the dumpster. Still, we didn't pause in our effort to flee. Seeing stars and my head throbbing, I hoisted myself over the edge of the trash receptacle and ran toward the truck. The dead in the distance suddenly looked much closer than they had from the roof and the truck much farther away. The monsters within the building were aware that we had run, the distraction leading to the ultimate demise of the weaker of the two. I could feel its rage. Instead of looking back to make sure Chanel was still with me, I kept my eyes focused on the truck and trusted that the footfalls that mingled with my own belonged to her.

From the reflection in the back truck window, I saw the misshapen form of the Hunter emerging from the building behind me. I could only assume that it killed whatever horror it fought inside the nursery. The truck was a mere two yards away and I didn't dare take my eyes off the vehicle. The stench of decay was overpowering. Reaching the pickup, I fumbled to open the door. My hand slid from the handle and hit the mirror with more force than was comfortable. Chanel ran into me in her own rush to enter the vehicle. I stepped aside just long enough for her to open the door.

"The truck's covered in blood," she huffed, struggling to get enough air.

"Get in," I urged.

My gaze focused on the Hunter, who in all its bloated glory bumbled toward us. One of its legs was limp, causing it to undulate as it made a sloppy attempt to run. I sensed from it both the sweet joy of victory over whatever it had fought inside the garden store and the sour desire to devour. I clambered into the truck before Chanel was in the driver's seat.

"It's different than other Hunters," I said quickly as I forcefully pulled the door shut behind me. "Start the truck and go!" I screamed.

Chanel's hands were shaking, causing a delay in inserting the key into the ignition. The Hunter was slow and not posing an imminent threat, but the horde of Roamers quickly approached, threatening to surround us. It seemed an eternity before Chanel finally turned the engine over. She stepped on the gas pedal, but the truck didn't move forward as smoothly as it should.

"The parking brake," she gasped.

A moment later she managed to dislodge the brake and the truck lurched forward. A thunderous screech shook me to my core. The effect inside my head was dizzying and I panicked. It was unlike any sensation I had experienced before.

"Zoe, what's wrong?" I heard Chanel ask.

I clutched at my head. It felt like a large fist was latched around my brain and I wanted to vomit.

"Zoe?!"

I clenched my teeth together and forced two words out. *"Keep...going."*

Whatever it was that had a hold of me was terrifying, and I knew on a primal level that it was by far the worst of the plague we'd yet to encounter.

"What's wrong?" asked Chanel.

"There's something waiting for us," I groaned. "It's in my head and hurts like a sonofabitch."

"I thought you stopped hearing them?" she asked.

"Yeah I did."

"Up there. See it?" she asked.

I looked in the direction she indicated. Roamers were beginning to cross the highway, directly in our way.

"Run them over," I half growled.

"Not them. We can take those out easily. Over by that pine tree. Do you see her?"

I strained my eyes. Both the tree and the figure were far enough away that it wasn't easy to make it out. It was the presence of pure white that drew my eyes. In a world ravaged by the dead, everything wears a coat of grime and white that pure is rare. The truck jolted when it hit one of the Roamers.

"Keep going," I said.

The faster Chanel drove, the worse the splitting pain in my brain got.

"Your nose," said Chanel as she ran into another of the dead.

I looked at her sideways.

"It's bleeding," she explained quickly.

I wiped the back of my right hand against my upper lip and inspected it afterward. It was smeared in bright red blood. Two more Roamers met their fate with our front bumper as I searched the distance for the lone figure again. I made an inhuman noise as my head filled with the thoughts of the creature topped in white.

You're ours.

The truck came to a screeching halt, throwing me into the dashboard. I had no idea what Chanel had hit, and I was dazed for a moment while the dust from the air bags settled.

"Chanel…" I groaned.

She didn't respond.

"Chanel…"

I scooted over toward the driver's seat and felt for her. She moaned when I found her arm.

"We have to move," I said quietly.

The minds of a hundred dead filled my head, and each of them was ravenous. One was commanding the others. She was stronger than any other presence I had ever felt, and she was evil. She wanted me. She wanted me alive. She had already told the others to take Chanel, to do what they wanted with her, but to keep me alive.

"I can't get out, Zoe," said Chanel with panic rising in her voice.

"You have to. They're gonna to surround us."

"No, I'm stuck. I can't feel my legs," she said as she started to cry. "You have to go…"

I ignored her and scooted closer to her. She swatted at me with one of her arms, and when I slid my arms around her to pull her toward my door she cried out sharply.

"Noooooo!" she yelled, shrill and pained.

"I'm not dying today, and neither are you!" I hissed as I pulled on her again.

In the distance an explosion rocked the air. Gunfire rang out immediately afterward. Someone yelled as another explosion rocked the truck.

"What the hell," I mumbled as I continued to struggle to free Chanel.

The maimed Hunter that was somewhere behind us yelled out in anger, or maybe in pain. Things happened so quickly. The passenger door flung open and rough hands found me. Not knowing if they were dead, alive, or had ill intentions, I fought back with all the strength I could muster.

"Fuck," a deep voice cursed. "Let me help you, lady! Brett, I have one of them!"

"Austen and Keelie better hold off these fucks," hollered a gruff voice.

I took a gamble and figured human was safer than the dead that now surrounded us. We had no other way out, so I stopped fighting the man and let him pull me from the seat of the truck to the ground.

"Chanel!" I screamed. "Chanel!"

"We'll get her if we can," said the man loudly.

Sporadic gunfire and unholy screams in the background rang out. Another explosion nearby caused my ears to ring. I looked at the man who stood next to me. He was short with cropped brown hair and a full beard. He wore a dingy t-shirt that I assumed was once white, camouflage cargo pants, and a yellow handkerchief dangled from his wide belt. Wrapped around his bicep was a bandage that desperately needed changing. He grabbed my arm and pulled me to the ground with him as shots found their marks far too close to us.

"Stay down until I tell you to run!" he shouted. "When I do, don't let go of my hand."

"I can't leave without her," I cried out.

I didn't get a chance to argue the matter. He firmly gripped my wrist with his hand and began to pull me.

"Run!" He yelled.

I ran, despite aching to know if Chanel had made it out or not. It was hard to keep up with the man urging me forward. The ground was uneven and I stumbled more than once. Each time, he kept a firm grip on my wrist. It was too dark to see where we were headed, and the moans of the dead were too close for me to really care.

"Get in!" yelled a woman gruffly.

Before I could argue, the man pulling me along lifted me off my feet and tossed me slightly upward, where more hands received me and pulled me into the bed of a pickup truck. Faces were distorted in the eerie red of brake lights. I counted five people in all, two of whom were busy acting as snipers.

"Did Bret get the other one out?"

"Haven't seen him yet," answered a boy who couldn't have been older than his teens.

"The Hag? Is it down?"

"Pretty sure Keelie took it out. Didn't you hear it screaming?"

"Yeah, but they scream like that all the time."

"Get her down!" yelled the same gruff woman.

"Get back," urged the man who had pulled me out of our wrecked truck.

I haphazardly made my way toward the cab of the tuck, careful to step over an assortment of tarps, weapons, and what looked like it may be a dead body stuffed into a duffel bag. Three other adults stood near the sides of the truck bed, shooting into the darkness. I ducked down.

"Watch for him, mate," said a thick male voice with a heavy Australian accent.

An unholy and inhuman scream came from somewhere behind me. The smell of gunfire burned my nose.

"I see Brett!"

"Keelie, get in the cab!" shouted the teen.

"Not yet!" the woman barked. "The Hag's still out there. I don't think the RPG hit it. We can't risk it following us."

"Sven, get the girl to the Armadillo! Keelie and I'll stay behind to wipe out the Hag."

The teenager, Sven, quickly went into action. Swinging his rifle to his right side, he held a hand out for me. I reached for the handgun I kept in my back waistband, only to find it missing.

"I need a gun," I said loudly as I took hold of his hand and jumped out of the truck bed.

Without hesitating, he pulled a pistol from a holster on his belt and handed it to me, grip first.

"Stay close," he said. "Head for the other truck, see the running lights?" he asked.

"Yeah."

. We ran toward the other vehicle. The ground beneath my feet shook as another explosion rocked in the distance, the resulting flash of light disorienting. I stumbled on the uneven ground, catching myself with my free hand and quickly up-righting myself. Several steps ahead of me, Sven stopped and turned to make sure I was still behind him. He nodded once and I caught a glimpse of something menacing in his eyes. The grin that spread slowly across his face sounded alarm bells in my head. Without hesitating, I ran toward him. He stood his ground, rifle raised. At the last moment possible, I slid toward him feet-first. His gun fired above me, the rounds making a closer call with my head than

I cared for. He fired the semi-automatic weapon again and I covered my head with my arms.

"Get up!" he yelled urgently. "There's more coming!"

I half scrambled to my feet and was half pulled by my shirt. I looked back only once, and saw a Roamer lying still; Sven had shot its head off. I had picked up on Sven's basic feelings. The connection was vague and unlike any other I had experienced, but I was sure now that he too was infected.

We ran the rest of the way to the truck the other man had called the "Armadillo." As we reached the very rear, I could see it was a metal box on wheels. There was too such smoke in the dark night air to see just how long the structure was, but I figured it was a semi. One of the barn-style doors on the back opened outward as we approached. I could barely make out a figure. Sven pushed me toward the person, who hoisted me up into the metal trailer.

"Get to the front. It's safer there," the man said.

"Sven, you too. We're about to roll out."

"Can't, boss. Keelie and Ed are still out there. I lost track of Brett."

"My friend Chanel," I gasped, my lungs irritated by the smoke and gunpowder in the air. "She was trapped in the truck."

"You're damned lucky we came across you," said Sven. "If anyone can get her out, it's Brett."

"Speak of the devil!" exclaimed the man standing in the truck's trailer.

Running toward the truck, a middle-aged black man carried Chanel over his shoulder in a fireman's hold, blood dripping down the front of his shirt.

"Chanel!" I cried out.

"Later," said Sven sternly. "Back up. We'll get your friend loaded in."

I nodded curtly and backed up to give them room.

"Tracy, grab her feet," said Sven.

The other man grabbed onto Chanel's legs as Sven wrapped his arms around her trunk.

"We gotta get outta here," said Brett as he jumped into the trailer.

"Who's in the cab?" asked Tracy as he laid Chanel down on the cold metal floor.

"Is she alive?" I asked, worried sick.

The men looked at me almost as if they had forgotten I was there.

"Yes. I think she's broken a leg, or maybe her pelvis. When I pulled her from the truck she lost consciousness. It's best for now."

"We need to get her back to Doc. He can help her," I said quickly.

Sounds of gunfire and horrific screams and wails continued around us. Sven pulled the back door to the trailer shut, bathing us in near complete darkness.

"Brett, who's in the cab?" asked Tracy a second time.

"Zander, as far as I know. Keelie promised his mom she'd keep him out of harm's way."

Tracy rushed to the front end of the trailer, cursing under his breath when he collided with something. He pounded his fist upon the bulkhead and within a brief moment the truck began moving. A light mounted to the trailer wall was turned on.

I knelt down next to Chanel and found her hand. She stirred and whimpered.

"Where are we going?" I asked loudly.

"We're heading toward Wenatchee. One of our scout teams went that way and hasn't come back."

"Our group's only about ten miles that way. I know they'll help look for your people, and I have to get Chanel to Doc."

Sven looked at Brett, who nodded. He looked back at me and seemed contemplative.

"They'll welcome us?" he asked.

"I know they will. Who knows, maybe your people are there?"

He sighed heavily. "Let me know where to go."

I explained the general route and what building to look for. The truck continued forward, tossing us about as it hit the slightest rut or bump. Chanel cried out a few times. The sound of gunfire ceased but the screams of undead…things…continued behind us for several miles.

"What was that thing?" I asked Sven.

"The Hag?"

"Whatever was wailing."

"We call them Hags. They scream like a banshee and look like the Wicked Witch of the West. You haven't come across them yet?"

I shook my head no.

"Consider yourselves lucky. They're the worst of the dead. We've been fighting them off for almost a year."

Tracy walked back toward us. "They seem to be migrating south. Maybe looking for food or warmer ground."

"It was white," I said.

"What do you mean?" asked Brett.

"Bright white. Like it was wearing a bright white hat."

"Some of them wear skins," said Sven, as if that explained everything.

"Skins?" I asked, needing clarification.

"Yeah. Some of the kids born these days are really fair. The Hags prefer them, seem to seek them out. I guess they wear what's leftover when they're done," elaborated Brett.

I felt the blood rush out of my face and my stomach formed a large knot. Now, more than ever, I just wanted to be home and with my husband.

CHAPTER 18

The drive back to our settlement was tedious. Chanel woke up screaming in pain and was inconsolable. I sat beside her, always holding her hand.

"We'll be there soon, Nell. Doc'll fix you up." I knew she loathed the nickname, but I hoped deep down it reminded her of home and how much she'd like to be there.

"It hurts so bad," she said, crying.

"I know. We'll be there soon and get you pain meds."

"Zoe, we need to know how to get to your place," said Brett. "I'm gonna knock for Zander to pull over and we'll get you up front so you can guide him."

"I need to stay with Chanel," I said calmly.

"No," said my injured friend. "You'll need to be in the cab so they see you. Otherwise they may turn them away."

I sighed, knowing she was right.

"Miss Chanel, when we pull over you'll have to be quiet. We can't attract the dead."

She nodded in understanding and bit her lip.

"Go ahead and let Zander know," said Brett.

"You got it," answered Tracy. He proceeded to knock loudly on the front of the trailer.

"How can he even hear you from back here?" I asked. Surely there was a gap between the tractor up front and the trailer that we occupied.

"He can't," answered the man.

"Zander's deaf," explained Sven. "The panel Tracy's beating on attaches to a light in the cab. When he hits it, the light flashes."

"Oh," I said. "That's clever."

"Thanks, it was my brilliant engineering," said Brett with a smile.

The rig slowed and came to a smooth stop. Brett opened the back trailer door and jumped down onto the highway. I leaned over and kissed Chanel on the forehead.

"I'll see you in a few minutes, okay? At home."

She nodded; I noticed that she was also shivering despite having a blanket over her.

"Let's go," said Brett.

I stood, feeling every stiff joint and sore muscle. Ignoring the pain, I moved toward the open doors and jumped out of the trailer. The minds of the dead who taunted me were distant. Brett escorted me to the passenger side of the rig, where he helped me up the steep steps to the passenger seat. I watched as he signed something to the teenager named Zander. The boy was fair and covered in freckles, his head topped with thick ginger hair. My thoughts immediately shifted to Emilie. He looked like he could have been her brother. He nodded to Brett, who turned to me.

"I just told Zander where we're headed and to pull off when you signal. Will he be headed right or left?"

"It's on our right."

Another set of hand signals relayed the information on to the boy.

"Just raise your hand when you see the right place, okay?"

"Sure."

Brett stepped down to return to the trailer. Before he could close the door I called his name.

"Brett?"

He looked up at me.

"Take care of Chanel?"

"Of course. Like she was my own daughter."

"Thanks."

He shut the door and left me with Zander, who saluted me with two fingers and smiled before waiting for his signal to proceed. Shortly after, the overhead light flashed on and off several times. Zander put the rig into gear and continued on.

The landscape was unfamiliar in the dark, so I tugged on Zander's sleeve to catch his attention. He looked at me quizzically. His speech was slurred, but he did his best to ask if we were there. I shook my head no.

"Slow down?"

He shrugged his shoulders and looked confused. I watched as he pointed to a small pad of paper attached to the dash, hanging from it was a pencil on a string.

I smiled at him.

I carefully scrawled a single word.

Slower

He nodded, and reduced his speed.

We rounded a bend, which seemed vaguely familiar, and one of the best feelings in the world overcame me. My husband. I could feel him in my soul. He was furious and terrified, but he was with me.

I tugged at Zander's sleeve again. When he looked over at me, I pointed to the right and held up my hand. I scrolled on the pad of paper again. *We're close.*

He nodded and slowed the rig further. Our settlement appeared without much notice, the headlights on the truck only reaching so far. Zander slowed as he pulled over onto the shoulder. Zander said something to me in sign language, and I was at a loss.

"This it?" he said aloud, still slurred.

I nodded yes and made a final note on the pad of paper.

Truck won't fit in the garage

"O-K" he said with some effort.

I managed to open my door despite it being heavy, and slid down to the earth below. My plan had been simple – go to the chain link fence and beat on it until one of the guards heard me. I didn't need to. Before I reached the barrier, I heard yelling.

"They're back!"

I didn't recognize the voice.

"Open the gate, now!" boomed Gus' voice.

The anger in his voice threw me off.

"Zoe!" he screamed. *"Zoe!"*

He reached the chain link before the guards were able to open it. His knuckles were white where he gripped the wire diamonds. I stayed back a few feet.

"Jesus Christ, woman! Why the fuck did you leave without telling me?"

"Calm down," I said forcefully.

"Calm down? *Calm down?!* Are you fucking kidding me? Zoe, what the *hell*?"

"Not right now. We need to get Chanel in to Doc. She's hurt really bad."

Gus pushed the button on a walkie talkie that was strapped to his belt. "Doc, we need you out front."

"No. Have him get pain meds ready first. She'll need them for us to move her."

At last the gate slid open to one side.

Gus stepped through as soon as he was able and wrapped himself around me. His embrace caused each ache and every pain to scream.

"What happened?" he asked, his tone just slightly softened. "You look horrible."

"I'll tell you later. It's Chanel that needs help."

"Tell me what happened," he said as I grabbed his hand and urged him to the back of the truck.

"These are good people. They need shelter for the night and help finding their scouting team. They saved us and got us back here. Chanel…she's hurt bad. They think a broken pelvis or something."

We heard Chanel's muffled cries. I could tell she was doing her best to stay quiet.

Brett and Tracy stood in the open end of the trailer as Sven held the door open from ground level. Gus immediately stepped up into the rig and knelt down next to Chanel.

193

"Hey sweetie," he said.

"Hey," she said, her voice strained.

"Sounds like you got roughed up."

"She crashed a truck and got pinned under the steering wheel," said Brett. "I barely got her out."

"It hurts, Gus," she said with a pathetic whimper.

"Doc'll be right out with something to take the edge off. Hang on, okay?"

She sniffled.

"Gus," I said to catch his attention.

"Ayup?" He was feeling along Chanel's sides, presumably looking for injuries.

"Have you seen Kendall? Did she come back?"

He paused and looked at me sideways. "No. You lost her? And where's Brenda?"

I began shaking. The reality of the situation was setting in, the adrenaline wearing off.

"Brenda's dead. We couldn't find Kendall. She might be back there still."

"You can tell me later after we get Chanel settled," said Gus. By his tone I knew that he had strong words for me later. "You need to head in and get cleaned up. Doc'll want to look you over after he takes care of Chanel."

"I'm not leaving her," I said firmly.

Olga appeared almost out of nowhere and jumped into action. "Doc's getting things set up in the infirmary," she announced. "I'm here with IV supplies and morphine."

"Thanks, doll," said Gus.

She set the supplies down by his knees. Gus didn't pause in his tasks, expertly inserting the IV in a span of less than thirty seconds.

"Hold the bag up?" he said to Olga.

She had already begun to do so. They worked seemingly flawlessly together.

"Can I do anything?" I asked.

"No," was all Gus said angrily.

He picked up an already-filled syringe and screwed it to the IV line before pushing the fluid in.

"Chanel, the morphine's already going in. I'm giving you a hefty dose, darlin', and you'll probably feel real sleepy just any second."

She didn't reply to him, but her breathing slowed and her shaking calmed. I took that as a good sign.

"Let's go," said Olga. "Doc's awaitin'."

"We can help carry her inside," offered Brett.

"Thank you kindly," said Olga.

Gus helped roll Chanel onto her side while Olga, Tracy, and Brett tucked a piece of thick canvas beneath her. Before long they had her on her back again, and the four of them lifted her rather easily. She moaned during the movement, but quickly settled.

I stayed far enough back to not be in the way. Many faces I recognized stood near the gate waiting for them to carry Chanel inside the perimeter. Zander stood in front of the semi-truck and waved a smaller pickup over. I had forgotten the rest of their group would be following us.

"Zoe, maybe explain to everyone who all these people are while I help patch Chanel up," Gus called back to me.

I watched as they carried her away, not quite sure what to do or where to go.

***

When I finally got to the infirmary, the door was locked. A note on the door read "patient inside, please come back another time." My heart sank as I heard Chanel scream on the other side of the door. Disheartened, I walked away and followed the hallway to the stairwell that led to our apartment above. One of the other gardeners, a young girl named Bethany, tried to catch my attention as I walked past, but I ignored her.

I got to our unit by muscle memory. I was tired, in pain, filthy, and my heart hurt for so many reasons. I let myself in and felt along the kitchen counter for our flashlight. I turned it on and walked to the bathroom, where I stripped out of my clothes and kicked them aside. I stepped into the wading pool and turned the hose on. As soon as I was wet, I shut the water off and lathered myself with soap and shampoo. I needed to cry but hadn't the energy. Wanting to curl up and die, I rinsed off quickly and wrapped myself in a bath towel. I left my hair damp and un-brushed, satisfied that it was at least clean. Making my way to the bed, I dropped my towel and curled up near the pillows. In contrast to the recent heat of the season, the night felt chilly. I grabbed onto the quilt and pulled a corner over myself.

***

I didn't hear Gus come in. I didn't feel him sit on the bed next to me. It was the sound of him crying gently that woke me up.

"Zo?" he called softly.

I opened my eyes. The apartment was pitch black.

"Yeah…"

He adjusted his position on the bed and settled in behind me, wrapping himself around me.

"Is she going to live?" I asked.

"I think so. Doc thinks it's the head of her femur that's broken. She'll be off her feet for a few weeks, but he thinks it'll mend. I thought you might be dead, I thought something horrible had happened. I couldn't handle that, love."

"I can feel you again," I whispered into the darkness. "I can feel you in my soul, Gus. I know how much you're hurting. I can feel it all."

"Then you can feel how much I love you."

"Yes."

"Please don't ever leave like that again."

"I just needed a change," I said.

His hands worked their way to my own.

"I know," he breathed against my neck.

His lips found my flesh and he hungrily tasted me. I turned to face him and buried my face into his chest.

"There's horrible things out there," I said.

"I know."

196

He continued kissing my neck softly and pulled me close.

"There's worse things than we knew."

"We'll talk about it tomorrow."

"I want to go back to the ocean," I said.

"You want to leave this place?" he asked, concern in his voice.

"I don't know. Maybe for awhile."

"We'll figure things out in the morning."

His lips found mine and I accepted his embrace, melting into him. That night we made love gently and sweetly, and like there may never come a tomorrow.

EPILOGUE

With morning brought sorrow. Chanel made it through the night, to my relief, but Kendall was located about a mile from home. She suffered a much worse fate, having been partially eaten and turned, searching aimlessly for a meal. The newcomers accompanied our own people in search of both her and Brenda as well as their scouting team. The truck we had come across, abandoned and covered in blood, was their scouting vehicle. The duo who had occupied it never were found. The conjoined twins in the ice chest were brought back for a proper burial. No one knew who they were or how they got there, but one of our own decided they needed to be buried.

Gus and I discussed the future, however long it may be. The ocean called to me. The beach was the last place I held Molly. Puget Sound served as the grave of my best friend, Emilie. I needed to sit and reflect. Together, we decided to leave the settlement and head northwest until we got to the sea. After describing the Hags to my husband, going to colder land seemed the best option. If we could get there before winter hit, we might be lucky and find something already stocked and secure. Maybe on another island.

***

Traveling, just the two of us, we grieved our lost children and friends. We found each other once again. We told one another that someday we'd go back to the settlement. The dead became sparse the farther north we went, but traveling also grew increasingly difficult. We carried what we could on our backs and rode bicycles until the terrain grew too difficult to ride. After that, our feet carried us.

We knew we'd found our new home when we reached a rocky beach with a lone dock leading to a small lake. A modest wood cabin sat tucked into the tree line and in the distance I could hear the nearness of the Pacific Ocean as waves rolled onto the beach.

"We could make it work," I said.

"Ayup."

"I'm tired."

"Me too, darlin'. Me too."

We stood hand-in-hand looking at the lake. It was a calm day, the sky overcast and threatening to snow. A fish jumped, leaving ripples in the otherwise still water.

Lightning Source UK Ltd.
Milton Keynes UK
UKHW042048050519
342144UK00001B/46/P